A Hot Mess

Edd McNair

www.urbanbooks.net

Urban Books, LLC
78 East Industry Court
Deer Park, NY 11729

ISBN 13: 978-1-60162-456-7
ISBN 10: 1-60162-456-5

First Printing July 2011
Printed in the United States of America

10 9 8 7 6 5 4 3 2 1

This is a work of fiction. Any references or similarities to actual events, real people, living, or dead, or to real locales are intended to give the novel a sense of reality. Any similarity in other names, characters, places, and incidents is entirely coincidental.

Distributed by Kensington Publishing Corp.
Submit Wholesale Orders to:
Kensington Publishing Corp.
C/O Penguin Group (USA) Inc.
Attention: Order Processing
405 Murray Hill Parkway
East Rutherford, NJ 07073-2316
Phone: 1-800-526-0275
Fax: 1-800-227-9604

CHAPTER 1

"Ooh, Boooby! Yes, yeeess! Suck on it. No, no! You gonna make me—Aaaaghh." Joy squirmed uncomfortably as Booby pulled his pinky finger out of her ass just when she pushed his head away.

Now here he come holding his dick in his hand, ready to fuck, she thought as he grabbed her and pulled her down.

Guiding his dick inside her, Booby placed his arms behind her knees and lifted her ass up so he could get deeper.

Joy grabbed her ass and spread her cheeks. It felt as if Booby had grown an inch longer. She knew she had him, from the expression on his face, so she made her pussy tighten, squeezing her hot, moist insides on his dick and pulling back.

Booby quickly got in her rhythm, praying not to lose the feeling he was experiencing. With no control, he arched his back, strained his neck, dropped his already heavy bottom lip, and let out a satisfying, "Aagh! Whoa! Damn! That was off the chain!"

"Did you enjoy yourself?" Joy asked, holding his face in her hands.

Booby was like a puppy, ready for her every command. "Yes, for real. Give me a sec, and we can do it again," he said, hyped.

"Not right now, baby. Let me rest. Shit, I know you got business anyway."

"Fuck that!" He grabbed her and lifted her entire 180 pounds on top of him, and slid back inside her. When he started pumping, his dick was already hard again.

"Yes, baby, that's what I'm talking about," Joy said as she placed her hands on his chest and began bucking like a horse. The friction between her legs began to send a chilling feeling through her body as she and Booby came again.

Booby eased to the side of the bed and stood up, gripping her ass, holding her with her legs still wrapped around him. He guided her to the bathroom.

"Put me down, boy. You know I'm too big," she said laughing. Joy was enjoying every minute of his attention. Nobody ever picked her up. Never.

Booby made his way back into the shower.

Joy grabbed her towel and wiped herself. She had major cleaning up to do before Andre came in Thursday. She threw on her robe and lit a Newport, walking downstairs.

Moments later Booby came downstairs, his Levi's hanging down low enough to show his Rocawear boxers.

Joy looked in his direction and caught the crisp, new butter Timbs scuffing her hardwood floors. He threw his wife-beater on and tossed the white tee across the arm of the chair. He leaned over and kissed Joy then fell down beside her and pulled out a Dutch.

"Hell naw, Booby! That nigga be back in a couple days. I got to let this house air out," Joy said, fussing.

"Get me something to drink. Kill that bullshit," he said, nudging her to get up.

"You trying to get me fucked up. Then what? What the fuck I'm gonna do?" She handed him a bottle of cold water.

Booby lit his Dutch then took the water.

"You really don't give a fuck, do you?"

"How long you been divorced?"

"Eight years! Thank ya, Jesus," she answered, waving her hand.

"How long we been friends?" he asked, passing her the Dutch.

Joy hit it a quick two times and passed it back. Smoking wasn't really her thing anymore. "Five years."

"How long we been fuckin'?"

"Four years."

"This is yo shit. That nigga gonna hold you down, not by choice, because he know you'll get another muthafucka in here real quick. You learned the game quick. You gonna keep your shit straight and never give the nigga the upper hand. Other words, I ain't worried about you being fucked up. Now, let me get some change." Booby pulled on the Dutch then held it out for her.

"I got a hair, nail, and pedicure appointment tomorrow. I took off. You need to be seeing me on something."

"Yo, I'm like that right now. Let me hold something. Gotdamn, baby!" he said, turning out his pockets, showing some change and weed.

"You ain't got no money, but you got all that new shit on, and you got weed. Please, nigga." She grabbed her Louis Vuitton bag and opened it up. Glancing inside, she said, "This all the cash I got on me," and handed him forty-five dollars.

"I'll run to the bank," he offered, trying to hold back the laughter, knowing what was coming next.

"I don't need a ride no gotdamn where. Boy, you lost," was all she got out before he busted out laughing, grabbing and hugging her.

"Shut up, boy! And stop playing!" she said, balling up her fist and punching him.

Booby caught her fist and pulled her to him and put his arms around her. She felt cuddly to him. He reached around and gripped her butt and pulled her to him. Then he leaned over and wrapped his arms around her waist.

He squeezed her, not so she couldn't breathe, but just enough to take her breath away, and he held her. She rested her head on his chest, his head on top of hers, and they held their embrace.

"Love you, Booby," she said and kissed him.

"Love you too, Joy. Believe that shit." He gulped his water down. "I'm out," he said, putting on his white tee and blue hoodie.

As Joy walked Booby to the door, he stared at her big ass that jumped with every move. He put his arms around her capacious abdomen, so he could just ride on her ass for a few steps. Then he reached around and pulled her robe, which fell open, and got a handful of forty-two-DD breasts. His dick instantly hard again, he pushed her against the wall, lifted the robe, and was back inside of her, enjoying the sight of her ass jiggling with every stroke. He grabbed her waist and began to slam his dick inside, fast and hard.

Joy began to weaken. Her thirty-four years versus Booby's twenty-eight was becoming a bit much in round three.

She allowed her experience to kick in. Placing her hands on the wall, opening her legs as wide as they could go, she tiptoed and pushed her chest down below her hands and stuck her ass out and up, exposing him to all of her.

"Oooh shit! Yes, baby!" Booby put his hands on the wall and started slamming dick so hard, he almost lost his balance, just before squeezing his arms around her waist, shaking. He came so hard, he fell to the floor and leaned back.

Joy went and got a hot, clean towel, came back, and Booby was snoring. He jumped when she placed the hot towel on his dick and began wiping him, but he quickly relaxed. Afterward, she wiped herself, gave him another hug and kiss, and he was gone.

Joy went and opened all the windows. Even though it was a cool evening in March, the house needed to air out. She sprinkled Carpet Fresh through her downstairs and vacuumed. She went around the house and lit her scented candles then ran upstairs to throw a load of clothes in. She pulled her sheets, towels, pillowcases, and washcloths to toss them in the wash then cleaned her room and bathroom thoroughly.

By the time she was finished, it was 8:30 P.M. She ran some bathwater, soaked for half an hour, and threw her load in the dryer. By 9:00 she was in front of the TV, with a glass of wine and her Newports, looking at *The First 48*.

"Now I can go back to the real world," she said out loud, retrieving her cell phone. She'd missed seven calls, four from Quandra, her daughter. "Hell no! I ain't babysitting for no gotdamn body!" *Sorry, baby girl. You had that baby. Now yo' black ass gonna keep him. Not tonight*, she thought.

"Malaina and Kim." She smiled. "Where the fuck they at?" she asked herself. Then she saw Loeh. "Loeh, Loeh . . . not tonight. You can't follow Booby. Y'all niggas trying to kill momma."

Joy laughed as she sipped her wine and looked around at her new town home. She couldn't believe the deal she'd gotten for $137,000. The town house was easily $180,000, but with all the foreclosures and bank-owned properties, her agent managed to work out a deal on this 1,600 square feet single-garage, three-bedroom, two-and-a-half bath with a loft.

As she dug her feet into the couch and wrapped herself up in her throw blanket, she heard the doorbell ring and a knock at the door.

"Oh God, please make them go away," she prayed out loud. "And even more, please don't let that person have a key," Just then she heard the keys in the door.

"Hey, Ma!" Quandra yelled. "Where you at?"

"Ma, where you at?" Quandra's little boy said, repeating after her.

"Up here," Joy said.

"Up here, up here," Quandra's son said, climbing the stairs.

"No, get him away," Joy said, covering up her head. Then she uncovered it just in time for him to dive in her arms. Joy hugged him tight. He was her heart.

"So what's up?" Joy asked. "What you been doing today?"

"Nothing. Went and bought him some new shoes."

"You always buying shit. Better put some money up. Y'all will be looking for it later."

"We all right. Dro buy all that stuff. He want him to have it." Quandra sat down on the other sofa.

"Q, I know Dro gives you money. I said for you to put some up for a rainy day. And why this boy up under me? He done took off his shoes and socks."

"He all right. We gonna stay here tonight. Andre be home Thursday night?" Quandra asked.

"Thursday, baby." Joy yawned. "You seen your daddy?"

"Yeah, I went by his house yesterday. You know he all right."

"I know damn well he is, fucking up my eleven hundred dollars a month. Yo' brother shit stopped soon as he turned eighteen, and you, soon as you got pregnant. Sorry-ass nigga!"

"No, he ain't. Daddy has always took care of us. You just lost him. Don't shit on him to me, Mommy. Please don't do that." Quandra looked at her moms with a please-don't-start-that-shit look across her face.

"What? You standing yo' ass up for that nigga? Where the fuck was he when we lost our house? We were at my momma's house, packed in a room, he couldn't come through. Where was he when we was in that fuckin' shelter downtown Norfolk? It was me, you, and Juan."

Quandra stared at her moms quietly as her mother released her frustrations, which never stopped.

"Who got us a house and provided everything for y'all?"

"You got a town house in Lake Edward, the worst neighborhood in Tidewater when we moved out there. I knew them niggas had lost their mind. Police in helicopters, police on horses, police on bikes, and them niggas never stopped hustling, shooting, and killing. You call that a home? You call that providing? I remember my dad taking us to buy us clothes, sneakers, drawers, panties, everything, because we were looking broke down, and all you could think about is the next nigga. Don't get me wrong, Ma. You got us out the shelter, kept some food around, but don't act like you did that much, Mommy." Quandra started eating chips and drinking her juice.

"Yo daddy brought shit because he had money, because he wa'n't giving me shit. I was out this bitch killing myself, scrambling, and you always saying I ain't do shit and telling me don't say shit on him. Know what? Fuck that sorry-ass, black son of a bitch, and I know he probably say the same about me," Joy said, raising her voice. She stared at Quandra, breathing hard as she got up, and began to head to her room.

"Mommy, you know what?" Quandra asked seriously.

Joy stopped in her tracks and turned to her daughter. "What?" she asked, frustrated and exhausted.

"He never says anything *against* you or *about* you. Never."

Joy turned and walked in her room and sat down. She pulled out her photo album and opened it. She smiled at the sight of her, Chanel, Tiesha, and Tanika, better known as Queen, standing in front of her building in Brooklyn.

Until she was twelve, Flatbush was all Joy knew. She and Chanel lived in Flatbush, off Lenox. Tiesha, Chanel's cousin, lived in Brooklyn, while Queen, Joy's sister, was from Canarsie. Their moms hung tight. They'd both had kids by the same nigga at the same time and had to come together to beat off the other bitches coming at them.

Joy remembered when she and Queen went to their moms and asked how they were sisters. Joy's moms would say, "The man ran the entire section of Bushwick. He was from the Virgin Islands. Pretty muthafucka." Then she would sigh, allowing Tanika's mom to finish.

"But he was very mean and vicious. He killed a lot of people, he hurt a lot of people, but he took care of a lot of people. When he got indicted on kingpin charges, we were both seven months pregnant. This nigga brought us together and told us both we were carrying his babies. We both loved him more than anybody has ever loved him, but he was being deported, never to return, and we needed each other."

"And he was right," Joy's mom would always add.

And through conversations overheard by Tanika and Joy, they found out that their dad had slung dick all over New York and had about nine kids.

When it somehow leaked out that he had left two of his baby moms $50,000 each, things got crazy. Joy's mom left Brooklyn and went straight to VA with her sister. Queen and her mom went to Connecticut, but within two years, they were in Norfolk living with Joy's mother.

Sadness crept over Joy's body as she thought about Tiesha, who was still in Brooklien. Last she heard, Social Services had taken her kids. That dope had her gone real bad.

Chanel had come down with HIV and was one of the baddest bitches in Brooklyn, hanging in the clubs, getting niggas' money anyway she could and giving them a real package in return.

But the tears filled Joy's eyes when she turned the page and saw Queen on her wedding day. Queen was Joy's maid of honor and had taught her so much, gave her so much strength.

Growing up in Brooklyn, their mothers ran the streets hard, in search of love and fun. That left Queen and Joy alone many nights. Queen was tall and thick, and Joy was short and thick, so sex came into the picture early. At 10 and 11, boys 13 and 14 was sexing them in the building somewhere. Nobody was there to stop them from being grown. They began to realize that the guys would buy them shit and give them money, with just the chance to get with them.

By the time they were twelve, their game was tight, and them fifteen- and sixteen-year-old niggas was coming off, because Queen and Joy was the shit.

Then overnight Queen was in Connecticut, and Joy was in Norfolk. Joy's mom stayed with her sister for a second out Tidewater Park, but the tight squeeze of Joy and her brothers, plus her aunt's three kids, made Joy's mother get their own apartment quickly.

That's when they ended up out Oakmont North, in the Norview section of Norfolk. And Joy would take Norview by storm.

Joy flipped the page and smiled again. Malaina, Joy, Buffie, Stacy, and Scheri, with "The Oochie Coochie Girls" written at the bottom of the Polaroid. She began laughing out loud.

She got up to go get her wine from the loft. She saw her grandson, but not Quandra. *Why she leave him on the couch?* she thought, as she lifted him with her free arm while holding her wine and glass in the other. She took him to the bedroom and put him down. She kissed him and rubbed his head then walked out, leaving the door cracked.

That's when she realized Quandra was gone and had left the bag by the front door. She went and got her phone and dialed Quandra's number, just to get her answering machine.

"Yo, this Q dog. If you my peeps, leave a message and give me a sec. If you not, I got the four pound for ya— You wants no part of this Brooklyn bitch! Now hang up, faggot!"

Joy looked at the phone, disbelieving her ears.

"Q, I got shit to do in the morning, and I'm out at eight. Don't make me fuck you up!" She hung up and made her way back to her room.

Joy poured herself some more wine and turned back to the photo album. "The Oochie Coochie Girls," she said, thinking out loud. She looked in the mirror, stood on her bed, and did the Oochie Coochie dance. She laughed so hard, she was out of breath.

She looked at Malaina and herself, the only two who had gone from size eight to size eighteen. Malaina lived in Oakmont North also, her and Scheri, who was from Atlanta.

Malaina's peoples were from Bed-Stuy. *That's why we got so tight, and still tight*, she thought. *Both big, both from Brooklyn.*

Then she looked at Buffie, who now went by Gwynn. Then at fourteen, size 10, body tight. Eighteen years later, and three kids, Buffie still a size ten, but much more mature.

Stacy joined the Army and had been, for eighteen years, stationed in Fort Sill, Oklahoma, and she never came home. The only one that ever heard from her was Gwynn.

Then Scheri got real sick after her second child. A tumor grew on her brain and had to be removed, only to leave her unable to do for herself. Thank God for Mrs. Wessonly. She was a godsend. She left her husband, moved in with her daughter, took care of her child, and raised her grandchildren.

CHAPTER 2

Damn! Joy thought, giving herself a mental note to stop by and see Scheri. She flipped the page, and the best times of her life flashed before her eyes as she stared at the picture of her and Minke, Malaina, Wiz, Queen, and LeMar.

Joy had just turned fifteen. Her and Malaina were coming home from Norview High School when Wiz and LeMar rolled up on them in a new Z28.

Wiz was in the military and had just come home and got his new car. He was on Malaina as soon as he saw her. She tried to shoot him down, but he was so silly, they couldn't stop laughing.

He parked his car and walked with them for about twenty minutes, trying to convince them to go to a cook-out with him and his friends. The girls finally agreed, then walked and joked with him back to his car, where LeMar sat patiently.

"Can you go get my cousin?" Malaina asked. "We were on our way to see her."

"Sure. Where she at?"

"Turn down there. She live in Wellington Oaks."

When Queen came out, LeMar's eyes lit up like a child's at a circus. Joy and Malaina were fifteen, but could pass for eighteen, but Queen was taller, darker, with long, thick hair, and her moms allowed her to wear makeup. All that, plus her thirty-six-D's and big, wide hips, made most older guys ignore her age and slight belly.

"How old are you?" LeMar asked.

"Twenty-two," she said easily, letting it roll off her tongue like it was the truth. "Why? How old are you?"

"Twenty-one, and my man Wiz, twenty." LeMar turned his head to Joy and Malaina. "What about y'all?"

"Eighteen, graduating in June," Joy said.

"Nineteen. Supposed to have graduated last year." Malaina smiled. "But you know."

They all started laughing.

When they arrived at the cookout, Wiz had Malaina's attention, and she was enjoying herself as he joked, laughed, and entertained, keeping her close to him. And Queen had plenty attention coming her way.

Joy watched as most of the men eased their way to her, realizing that the perfect size eight wasn't what always got attention, but rather the ability to talk, flow, and flirt with the best of them. So even though Joy's body was tight and her light brown complexion, long hair, and natural beauty gave her an exotic look, as if she was mixed with something, she let it be known her peoples were as black as they came, but were just blessed with enhancing features. Not to mention, she still had the New York attitude and hadn't yet met the country nigga who could break it.

Joy had fucked with three niggas since being in VA. A nigga from Norview who was getting it with coke, a dude from Chesapeake into counterfeiting—she never trusted his money, so that fell short—and then D-Nell from Lake Edward. All these niggas paid like they weighed, straight hustlers, but Joy had started catching feelings over that Beach nigga, D-Nell, until he caught that murder charge and disappeared out her life. Since then, nobody had come close.

***

Joy sipped her wine and flipped the page. A feeling came over her body that she hadn't felt in a long time. It was from the sight of Minke with his arms wrapped around her the night of the cookout.

That day Joy remembered, she sat watching her sister Queen work the crowd. She sat up straight with her drink in her hand in her white tee, snug Levi's and new white kicks. She was about ready to go, until she heard four dudes coming in the backyard, one yelling, "Brooklyn."

She turned her head to watch the people show love. Two of the guys looked kind of grimy, but Minke and his boy Hitler were dressed in new shit, with jewels on from neck to wrist. She checked their style and felt back at home. She scanned the crowd and saw Queen talking to LeMar. Then she caught the dude who was reppin' Brooklyn coming her way.

"What up, ma? My name Minke," he said, with his hand out.

She looked into his low, slanted eyes, which he tried to hide behind the navy blue NY Yankee fitted that was pulled real low. She caught the white teeth, full lips, shadowed beard, and was instantly feeling this six foot one, skinny-ass nigga.

"Alecia. Nice to meet you, Minke." Alecia was her real name, and she used it with a nigga she liked.

"Damn, girl! You took my fuckin' line."

"Come with another one then. Been down here too long. Losing your edge. Unless"—she turned her head—"unless you one of those fake New York niggas."

"What you mean, ma?" Minke asked, admiring her style and sassiness. "Where you from?"

"Brooklyn. Flatbush," she said proudly. "And you?"

"Fort Greene. I am Brooklyn, baby, born and raised."

"So what got you in VA? I know this shit slow to you."

"Yeah, but I'm in school here. I came down here to go to Norfolk State. I'm a junior."

"So, if you go to school, why you looking like you running the city," she said with a smile.

"Come on, ma, I just told you I'm a Brooklyn nigga. I'ma get it if I got to rob and steal," he said with a slight grin. "Just like Uncle Murda."

"Who?"

"Maybe you been down here too long." Minke laughed.

"And who rolling with you?"

"You now. I came here because my man had something to do with it."

"Well, me and my cousins was asked, so we rode out here with Wiz and LeMar.

"Yeah, Wiz my man. So what's up with you, Alecia?"

"Tell me, Minke," she said with a smile.

"Let's go walk on the boardwalk, hand in hand, and act like we on Coney Island," he said with a bright, irresistible smile.

She looked at him with slight disappointment on her face. "I can't just bounce with you like that."

"Why? Tell me why, and I'll make it good. I want you to roll with me. I'm feeling you, for real." Minke looked at Alecia with a serious face, shaking his head and licking his lips.

"I got my sister and my cousin. We don't leave each other," Joy said seriously.

"We can all go, ma. You straight. Let me introduce your girls to my son. Yo, H, come here." Minke signaled his man.

Queen and Malaina had seen Minke talking to Joy, and soon as he called his man, Queen eased away from the other cats and was making her way over to Joy. She had learned a lot about niggas in her young years, and two on one was not about to happen.

"So what's up, Joy?" Queen asked, coming up beside her sister, staring at Minke and his boy.

"This is Minke and Hitler," Joy said, pointing at the dudes in front of her. "And this is my sister Queen and my cousin Malaina," she said as Malaina walked up.

"We all out in a few." Joy looked at Queen. "We gonna ride down the beach."

"Who the fuck these niggas? And we going where?" Queen asked in her hard New York accent, so they would know she wasn't from down South.

"Hold your mouth, ma. Watch when you speaking to a gangster." Hitler smiled, revealing his gold teeth. "Don't let the smile catch you slipping." He stared at Queen.

Queen never blinked as she stared back into Hitler's eyes. "No, don't *you* let the young faces fool ya. We seen your game, we know your game. Don't take us for one of these country-ass VA bitches," she said without smiling. "And I ain't smiling, so you know that it ain't a game." She kept staring Hitler down.

"This ain't a game. We just wanna chill, create some fun. Niggas ball like that all day," Minke said, looking at Joy. He was trying to ease the shit-talking between Queen and Hitler before it escalated to an argument. He was feeling Joy and spending some time with her was his mission.

"We gonna holla at my mans and them then we out. All of us," he said, hitting Hiltler and walking off.

They watched as the two stylish niggas walked off.

An hour later, Minke walked towards the gate to exit. He looked over at Joy and Malaina, and signaled for them to come on, pointing his fingers to the front.

Queen had started talking to some other guy. When she saw Joy and Malaina going to the front, she looked over to see Minke, Hitler, and the other guy that came in with them standing by the front gate. She signaled to her sister that she was coming, allowing her new friend to talk.

Hitler looked at Minke with a look of confusion and smiled.

"Where you from, son?" Minke asked, smiling.

With that, Hitler walked over to Queen and whispered in her ear, "We out now." Then he leaned back and stared in her eyes.

"I said I—"

"Your conversation is done," he said. "This is my girl, duke," he said turning to the dude she was talking to. He looked back at Queen. "And I'm not smiling, so that you know exactly what it is."

"Nice meeting you," the guy said, extending his hand to Queen.

Hitler pushed dude's hand down, looked at him, and placed his hand on Queen's waist. The guy moved on, and Queen walked towards the front.

As they walked out to the front, Queen looked at Hitler as they approached Minke. "I ain't your girl," she said, staring at Hitler as he approached his burgundy 325 BMW with the slight tint, wearing New York tags. "Don't you ever do no shit like that again."

"You are my girl. Now get the fuck in the car, before you end up in the trunk," he said, opening up his door and getting in.

Minke started laughing as he hit the alarm on the pretty canary-colored Milano.

"Nigga, you done lost your mind," Queen said, opening the door to the BMW and getting in.

Malaina and Sizemo jumped in the back of the BMW. "Guess we rolling over here," Malaina said.

"Glad of that, the way this man talking," Queen said seriously. Then she looked at Hitler as he started the car. He stared back at her. "So how many bitches been in your trunk?" She smiled.

"I don't know. Got to count the blankets in the back, see how many left." Hitler smirked, pulling off behind the Milano.

Joy looked at Minke as he drove the foreign car and leaned back like he was the coolest nigga, in complete control. "So, your boy was just joking, right? My sister hard as they come, because we've been through some shit, but she's been through much more. Take a special type dude to get her attention."

"She all right. He like her. They just got to feel each other out," Minke said. "Now tell me about yourself, Alecia."

"What you wanna know?" she answered softly, wondering what he was trying to pull out of her.

"Just want to know who you are. I'm feeling you. We only talked a little, but I'm looking at you like I'm gonna lock your ass down." Minke glanced at her.

Alecia smiled. She was already feeling him. All he could do was enhance the feeling or totally fuck it up—no in-between. She began talking as they hit the interstate, headed to the oceanfront.

CHAPTER 3

Joy turned the page of her photo album. She smiled at the pictures of her and Minke leaning against the Milano as they stood in front of Dairy Queen. Then she looked at the pictures of Queen and Hitler. After they got past the arguing, they became inseparable, just like Minke and herself.

Her eyes moved to the dry picture of Sizemo and Malaina. Malaina didn't feel him. She still had her mind on Wiz, who had brought them to the cookout. Malaina just didn't want to kill the opportunity for Queen and Joy to get with some real niggas. That was her style, roll with the flow.

She looked at the next picture that her and Queen had taken a year later at their seventeenth birthday party, where they had a cookout at Wiz's house.

Wiz was from New York also, but he'd been living in Norfolk since he was twelve. His parents had moved from Jamaica, Queens to Norfolk. He always traveled back and forth to New York, and never lost contacts with his roots there. When he got into Norfolk State, he came across some New York cats that were getting it, so he thought he could save a trip, not money. But it wasn't until he ran into Minke that his hopes came alive. Minke was hustling with a Brooklyn team that had come down from Bed-Stuy and had set up shop and was doing it big.

Wiz knew Hitler's man, Sleepy. When Sleepy ran into Wiz, it was over a bitch named Shaqvelle that was going to Norfolk State. Sleepy had fell in love with the pussy, while Wiz was just hitting.

Sleepy, with the 9mm in his waist, waited outside Shaquelle's door to confront Wiz. He froze as the familiar face came his way.

"Wiz?"

"Sleepy?" Wiz asked surprised.

They hugged.

"Yo, you fuckin' Shaquelle?" Sleepy asked.

"Fuckin' the shit out of her," Wiz said proudly. "Oh! Shit! That's you, son?"

"I been fuckin' with that bitch for about a year," Sleepy said to Wiz. "I was gonna lay a nigga down tonight. I was feeling this shit."

"Well, guess what, son? We go way back, and if she was worth shit, I would step back and say go for it. But grab your heart, my nigga. Bitch suck mad dick. Then I twist her ass every way but loose. And it ain't only me and you." Wiz smiled. He could see the hurt in Sleepy's eyes. He knew Sleepy was one of those wild niggas, quiet, low-key, but treacherous.

"I was feeling her, Wiz."

"So you go home, son. Get your mind together, get your heart together. Then come back and fuck the shit out her thick ass. Come on, man, let's go." As they eased away from the building, Wiz asked, "What the hell you doing in VA?"

They caught up, and Sleepy introduced him to Minke. Wiz knew how to move, and hustling was his thing. Him and Minke became tight, and money was being made. So when Minke found out that Malaina was feeling Wiz, he was all right with that.

After a year Malaina and Wiz were dating seriously, and he was treating her like a princess. Queen was serious with Hitler, who was controlling her in every way. Joy was still chilling with Minke at his apartment every day, and was six months pregnant. When Minke found out Joy was seventeen, he was totally shocked, but his love for her was unimaginable. He had fallen hard for her, and all he wanted was for her to feel loved and secure.

Joy frowned at a photo of Hitler and Queen. He loved Queen with a crazy, controlling love, but she was never scared of him. He gave her the world, but beating her ass was a regular. She turned the page to see pictures of herself and Minke on their wedding day. After the birth of their son, he was feeling so much love and closeness, he married her at seventeen, with her mom's consent. Queen was her maid of honor, and Sizemo stood as Minke's best man.

That was when Joy realized who was who. Minke and Sizemo were moneymakers, and Hitler, a Jamaican in the States illegally and with a don't-give-a-fuck attitude, was their connect. Hitler made Sleepy his enforcer, but because of his love for murder, he ran tight with Sleepy.

She turned the page, feeling her eyes getting heavy, but the pictures taken two years later gave her a big smile. That was the happiest time of her life. She was eighteen with two kids living in her three-bedroom, two-bathroom home with a gated yard and garage. It was 1991, and the year had just started. Malaina and Wiz were at their new home because they had the kids and no sitter, along with LeMar and his girl Taniesha. All of them would be graduating from Norfolk State in the spring.

Joy missed Queen, but her and Hitler decided to do the new year in New York. That would be the happiest time of her life and the worst. She remembered the call they received on January 3, 1991 at 4 A.M. Minke's phone went off, which it never did at that time.

She stared over at Minke when he got the news that they found Hitler in his new Q45 shot up. He'd been hit seven times from the fifteen shots that ripped through his car as he sat at the light on Utica and East New York. The unknown woman that sat in the passenger side was later identified as Queen. Five of the fifteen shots had hit her at point-blank range. She never had a chance.

Tears formed in Joy's eyes and said a pray. Through her ordeals, she had come closer to God, but she knew she wasn't where she should be, but was trying to get there.

She said a prayer for her family, and for Scheri, and ended it by saying, "Watch over Minke, God. Watch over Minke."

Joy knew down inside that when Hitler and Queen got killed, something inside both of them had died. Queen was her sister, which said it all. But Hitler was more than Minke's connect. They'd grown up in the streets of Brooklyn from six years old.

Hitler and his family had moved to BK straight from Jamaica. His mother and four boys moved in the building right across from Minke's family. At six they began to hang, by eight, Minke had taught Hitler more English than he knew. By twelve, Minke had learned to talk and speak patwa, so if he wanted you to think he was Jamaican, you would.

By sixteen, Hitler had made his name, with killer instincts and the rude boy attitude, but Minke was more laid-back. He moved slow, moved smart, and only told Hitler about niggas fucking up, if necessary. By eighteen, Hitler was making major moves down the East Coast—Baltimore, Norfolk, Carolina, and Atlanta—while Minke was still making moves, and plenty of money right in Brooklyn. He was gonna go to college in the city. He wasn't trying to leave because his money was flowing right.

One day when Hitler was home, he told Minke that wherever he went to school, he would make sure he was okay, so go ahead and apply. Minke checked into some schools and had always heard New York niggas talking about VA. So he checked out Virginia Union in Richmond, and Hampton University in Hampton, and Norfolk State in Norfolk. After Minke hollered at Hitler, Hitler told him he didn't care for Richmond, but he liked Norfolk.

The following semester, Minke enrolled at Norfolk State University. Two months later, Hitler hit the scene. People had already begun to take notice of the slim, dark-skin nigga always wearing the Yankee fitted pulled low, and driving the bright yellow Milano. So when Hitler hit the scene with the BMW 740 with New York tags, niggas knew the kid with the yellow Milano was well connected.

Minke ran with Hitler hard for the first semester, making big-boy moves, doing big-boy things. By the end of the semester, they had three of the downtown projects locked: Tidewater Park, Youngs Park, and Grandy Park, all with New York coke and heroin. Hitler had set it up to get rich, but Minke wanted something else. He didn't trust Norfolk for dealing coke, and always told Hitler it was too small, but Hitler said it was easier to take over, so he did.

Minke came back to school second semester and got him an apartment in every project Hitler did and a couple more. Then he set niggas up in each apartment, distributed the thirty pounds of weed he'd brought in, as well as the twenty pounds of hydro and the fifty pounds of chocolate Thai. He had weed spots from Park Place to Reservoir, which he locked down smoothly, and his shit would run for years to come.

Two years later, Hitler and Minke met Queen and Alecia. And Wiz, who worked for Minke, met Malaina. Two years later, he married Malaina and gave her three kids.

Minke gave Alecia a life she could only dream about and more. Gave her two kids and loved her like she could never imagine. But Hitler and Queen had a crazy love-hate relationship.

Minke and Hitler's family always wondered why Hitler was caught in East New York. They'd never ventured over there too often. It would be five years later before the truth would come out and destroy their life.

CHAPTER 4

Joy shook her head at the expression Minke had on his face as he came through the door. She didn't know at the time why he didn't want her to pick him up at the airport.

"Come over here, baby," she said, walking up to him, allowing the dark green silk robe to swing open so he could see the short, dark green nightie with the spaghetti straps, that was cut low and showed all her cleavage.

"What up, ma? What's the deal?" Minke said coldly, not hugging her back. He dropped his bag and made his way to the kitchen.

"Hold up. You been ghost for four days, and come in this bitch with attitude? I got the kids in bed, got your Dutch already rolled, got wine and shit laid out, and you go shitting on me?"

"Alecia, you know I just came from New York. You know we had the thing for his memorial."

"And it's been six years now. I lost my sister too, but that can't dictate our lives now," she said, getting even more upset.

"I ain't with all this shit, yo. Fuckin' blow out these candles and turn on some gotdamn light." Minke pulled a bottle of Moët from the refrigerator. He popped the cork, and excess bubbly ran on his plush, light-blue carpet.

"You fuckin' up, Minke. You lost your damn mind."

"Fuck this shit, all this shit, when it come to my peoples!" he yelled. Then he turned the bottle up to his head.

"I'm going upstairs," Joy said.

For real, she hadn't seen him like this but a couple times, and each time she seen murder. Being with him, she seen the same shit she'd grown up around, and more. Ever since Hitler had died, Minke had taken on Hitler's roll in every way. His fuse was always short, but now it was shorter. He was always quick to pull his burner at the right time, but now he pulled it fast at anytime, with one in the chamber, safety off. Ready!

"You ain't goin' no muthafuckin' where!" he yelled as he threw the champagne bottle through the forty-two-inch Sony television that sat in the black lacquer entertainment center.

Joy's heart began to beat harder and then faster. She grabbed her chest but couldn't move. But the second try was different. She shot for the stairs, with him on her ass, skipping the first three and never slipping as she made it to the bedroom and slammed the door. But her security came crashing down, just like the door off the hinges.

"What did I do? What did I do?" Joy cried as she jumped on the bed on her knees, her arms extended and palms up, begging for an explanation.

"I seen my girl Nikki from the East side. She was at Hitler memorial. She telling me—"

"Who the fuck is Nikki?" Joy yelled.

"Your fuckin' cousin. Nicholy Foxx, Nikki the nigga. Bitch get money like a nigga, down for anything—boosting, credit cards, setting niggas up. Then she turned into a stripper at night. You know who the fuck I'm talking about. Play stupid if you want to."

"I haven't seen Nicholy since I left New York. And even then we didn't fuck with her. She was into all kinds of shit."

"Well, Queen got with her—your sister Queen, if you forgot her. And they got those niggas in your old building, Redd and Paco, to get my dude. Queen told them when she was gonna get him to bring her through, and that he would have at least two hundred fifty stacks in the back. What she didn't expect was, they killed her for her cut. And know what? Nikki told them to."

"What?" Joy's eyes widened.

"Yeah, Nikki told me all her shit that you knew, Alecia. You knew this shit and didn't tell me. You my wife. People could have thought I was involved. You let me go out there not knowing, and that could have gotten me killed."

"I never knew if it was all true. I wasn't gonna bring chaos, not knowing if there was any truth to it." Joy knew she was wrong.

"When?"

"When what?" she asked, confused.

"When did you find out?"

"I got a call from Nikki two years later. She was drunk and crying at the club, but she ain't say shit about her involvement."

"Naw, I got that from Winner, old man Winner."

"He still around, gettin' high?" Joy asked, sitting back on her feet.

"He was there when Nikki asked Redd and Paco. Queen said she would give them fifty thou to split, and she would take the rest, and they agreed. But Nikki told them that she'd let them split one hundred thou, and she'd take one fifty.

"And what Nicholy say?" Joy was furious.

"Bitch shouldna been in the car, and laughed. Now that's some shit for ya." Minke walked back to where the door used to be.

"I'ma kill all them muthafuckas, word on my mother! They gonna see me," Joy said.

Minke stared at Joy, the love of his life. He loved her with all he had in him, but questions ran through his mind. *Did Queen tell her about this? Was she in on it? Had she been fucking with Nikki?* Minke had never doubted her. He never felt he had a reason, and no matter how hard he tried to look at her as his sweet, loving, innocent wife, he now saw a woman who would lie and keep things from him. And he hated that feeling.

"Paco and Redd, dem dead. Me cut 'em up real good for Hitler, real good. Nikki gonna get hers. But I'm gonna tell you, Alecia . . . I never expected nothing to go on and you know and not tell me. I'm your husband, you are my wife. You question my love and loyalty to you and my family because you thought I wouldn't understand. Now you got me doubting and questioning you," Minke said, a sad look on his face.

Joy sat on the bed with tears in her eyes. She couldn't believe what she was hearing after she'd given her all.

"I've loved the shit out of you since we've been together, gave you my everything. How could you say that?" she yelled as he made his way down the stairs.

Minke sat on the couch, lit his Dutch, and leaned back. The more he thought about things, the more upset he got, but the smooth-burning chocolate Thai stopped him from wilding out.

Joy cried and explained until Minke decided to leave. He had to fight to get out the door, and left her lying on the cold hardwood foyer, crying her heart out.

He returned days later, and it started.

Over the next several months, Minke began to treat her as if she was just another woman he fucked with, staying away for days at a time. And his patience was short when it came to her. He began to verbally abuse her because of her weight change. Then he went from making love and not being able to stay off her to her pleading, almost begging him to please her.

After almost a year of being treated like shit, Joy began to pull herself together for her kids. She realized Minke was too far gone to be reeled back in, so she slowly stopped calling his phone so often, stopped catering and waiting up, and went on with life, taking care of her kids.

Minke realized the change in Joy's routine. Thinking she was fucking around, he came harder at her. His disappointment changed to a dislike, and because of the way she began to ignore him, hate seeped into his heart and mind. He moved all his money, so she had none, and he let all the utilities go off.

The last straw was when he took her truck and drove it to New York. Then he called her and told her it was stolen. He came back got his car, and she didn't see him again.

Joy was humiliated and hurt as she and her kids were put out of her home that Minke had allowed to go into foreclosure. She couldn't stop the tears from rolling as she threw her last few things in her moms' car and they rolled away from her home.

"I don't believe this, Mommy," Joy cried. "I can't believe this shit. I was good to him."

Her mom said, "Go ahead, baby. Cry your heart out. Shed all those tears."

"Stop at the pay phone," Joy said before they reached her moms' house.

"Yeah, call him one more time, say all you gonna say," her moms said, knowing she was gonna call Minke.

Joy dialed Minke's number. She hadn't spoken to him in weeks. He wouldn't answer her call, knowing an argument was on the other end.

This time, surprisingly, he answered on the second ring. "Yeah. Who's this?"

"Didn't call to fuss. Just wanted you to know they foreclosed on the house and put me and your kids out on the street. I can see you leaving me, but your kids didn't deserve this. And they don't deserve to be in a shelter. All you had to do was walk away, just leave. I got nothing. Can't get no lower. But you watch me, nigga. I shedded my last tear, my last muthafuckin' tear, over you," she said with a smirk she let him hear. "Believe that."

"Fuck you and them kids, bitch!" Minke hung up.

Joy's heart stood in place. It didn't fall and hurt like it usually did. She slowly walked back to the car.

"It's done, girl. Get your shit moving and go ahead without that nigga," her moms said. "You can only stay with me one night, Alecia. It will be faster getting a place if you and yo' kids went."

"Mommy, I'm good," Joy looked at her moms with hurt in her face, but her heart in place. "Carry me downtown. We goin' in tonight. I'm gonna be fine."

"Damn right, you gonna be fine. Hold your shit in place and your head up. Now you will always know— one, never put your all into a man, and two, always have your own to fall back on," her moms told her. "What he say anyway?"

"Fuck me and the kids."

"Baby, you just learning how cruel men can be. When a nigga broke, he act the fool, when he got dough, he even worse. Get yourself together and find you a nigga with a regular life."

They rode in silence until they pulled in front of the shelter, where Joy would spend the next three months living in conditions far worse than she was accustomed to. She was hurt and confused, but she saw much more confusion and strain in her children's eyes. That was when she knew it was all on her.

Like she'd seen so many women do, she had to provide and make a way for her and her kids, so she found a job. With no transportation, the city bus became her friend. She rose early and got her kids straight. Performing her duties throughout her day allowed days to pass by without the stress of wondering what tomorrow would bring.

Joy couldn't believe the day she got the call from housing authority. Grinding for months, they had given her a date then shot down all her spirits. She sat on her cot with her kids close by, hurt, sad, and angry. She'd been sweet and passive her entire stay, so when one of the homeless people in the shelter tried to borrow without asking, something in her snapped, words were said, and in seconds, all the frustration that had built up in her exploded. And she was that wild, crazy, city bitch that people speak on.

Joy sprang from the cot to the intruder and was going hard until she was pulled off. Her daughter stood crying as her son stood firm, looking at his mom break this bitch down. Suddenly, Joy broke loose and grabbed a hard-cover Bible and charged at the sizeable woman, bringing the spine of the Bible across her nose. Blood splattered as Joy began throwing a flurry of punches.

This time she was grabbed and thrown to the ground until the police arrived. The other woman was hurt bad.

Joy looked up at her kids. Her son held his sister tight, keeping her from losing control, or more so trying to calm her down. She could see the anger in his glassy eyes at the men who were restraining his mother.

When he heard her yell from the knee in her back and saw her eyes fill with tears, he grabbed his lunch bucket and, with all his might, swung it, coming across the man's head, striking him in the corner of the eye and then again across the forehead. The man fell off Joy, grabbing his head. Without thinking, he jumped on the other man, but he was no match.

In seconds Joy was on him too, throwing blows, as her son held on the stranger's neck for dear life. After it was finally broken up, Joy was restrained and taken to Norfolk City Jail, from where they called her mother and, as first of kin, released all Joy's belongings and kids to her.

CHAPTER 5

Joy flipped the page. Reflecting on one of the most trying and hurtful times in her life wasn't easy. She looked at the girl sitting beside Bugg. It was her and Bugg on her mother's couch drinking. She looked like she would squish Bugg, a slim six foot one, 135-pound dude. After giving birth to her daughter Quandra, she'd shot up five sizes, not to mention her breasts had blown up. She didn't know how to really handle the weight, so she wore sweats and t-shirts, or big, flowing dresses.

She turned back a couple pages to the pictures at her son's first birthday party and stared at herself in the picture. "Thirty-six-DD, twenty-six waist, thirty-eight hips, size ten. Damn, I was a bad bitch! Hoes couldn't fuck with it," she said out loud.

But then those thoughts quickly washed away.

When Joy was released from jail, she had to stay with her moms. Her friends were her friends, but nobody opened their door, except her moms, who allowed her and her kids to occupy a room, leaving her moms on the couch most of the time.

The second night she was there, her moms sat her down. "I know your situation and I want you to get yourself together, but as long as you and them kids running my bills up, you got to pay your way." Her moms sipped on her Skyy vodka.

"Got you. I work, and I got you. I appreciate it. Give me a month or two, and I will have my own. I won't get comfortable," Joy said with attitude, never looking at her mom. She sipped on her Grey Goose and went back to doing her nails, mask on her face, and listening to Mary J.

"So when you gonna have some money?" Her mom lit a Newport. "Ain't no food in here, and those kids need to eat."

"I ain't got shit today. Friday I get paid. They'll eat fuckin' oatmeal and sandwiches," Joy said. *We're in a nice, quiet, comfortable, clean place. Now be grateful.*

"Well, I'm going to the store, so they can have a nice breakfast and lunch. You need to go get them signed up for school first thing in the morning."

"I know. You gonna take me, right?"

"No, you can go and bring my car straight back. I got things to do," her mom said, getting her keys.

"What you cookin' this late?"

"Shrimp and fries. I'm hungry."

"Hurry up. Me too," Joy said, smiling as her mom went out the door. It was the first time she'd smiled in a while and didn't have to force it.

For the next year, her mom made it comfortable for her grandkids, but hell on Joy. Every time Joy tried to save a penny, her mother had an emergency come up. Joy always gave a hand and gave more than she should've, but it was never enough. She didn't get peace until her pockets were dry and she was begging for bus fare or a ride to work.

She looked back down at the picture. She looked at her hair that was undone and her big, short, flowy dress, no makeup. She looked like a hot mess, but Bugg was right there up under her like a little puppy.

When she'd moved in with her mom, she wasn't computer literate, but after staying with her moms a short while, she built a Myspace site and started hearing from longtime friends. That's how she'd met Bugg, who she knew from middle school.

He'd had a crush on her, just like the other guys, because she was from New York. So when he appeared at her house after they'd caught up on life, the extra weight and other changes never made a difference. He wasn't doing nothing with himself and was still undesirable, but he kept her high and drinking. And he was there to give her rides to work, and to talk to when nobody else was there. He spent many evenings at her mom's eating, drinking, snacking, and being social. Moms loved him because he brought liquor when he came, and was there to help her daughter out.

One Friday night they sat up looking at movies, and everyone else was 'sleep. Joy herself fell asleep, and was laid back on the sofa. Bugg sat in the chair opposite her, staring at her exposed thigh, as her gown rode up, giving him a tempting view.

He'd tried many times to fuck Joy, but she never gave in. This night he decided to allow the tequila to take control and give him the courage he lacked otherwise. He leaned over and fell to his knees and buried his face in her crotch. As she began to stir, he moved her panties to the side quickly and began licking and sucking her love like no tomorrow.

Joy, who hadn't been touched in months, gasped at first. She began to push his head away at the moment he found her clit.

Bugg quickly took the enlarged clit into his mouth and began sucking and flicking his tongue across the little pearl ball. The force of his head being pushed stopped. Then he felt her fingers open, and her warm hands just sat on his bald head, as he sucked and licked ferociously, until her legs opened wider. She finally relaxed and allowed him to finish.

Bugg smiled. He slowed down and ate her until she shook and tried to push him away, but he grabbed her wrists and continued lapping up every drop of her cum.

Bugg tried to fuck, but it was a no-go. She wasn't attracted and never wanted to allow herself to get that desperate again.

A couple months later, after she and her moms got into a big argument over money, she came home from work, and her moms had her bags, her kids, and all her other shit bagged up and at the front door. With nowhere to turn, Bugg was right there to take her to his house, which he opened up to her as if she was his wife and those were his kids. And he allowed her to drive his hooptie. In return, she played wifey, cooking, cleaning, washing, and sharing his bed. Joy disliked it, but she was learning to deal with life and use her assets.

Joy poured the last of her wine into the glass. She was about to fall asleep when she flipped the page and saw the picture of herself standing beside her new used green Hyundai, and her roommate Tamil standing beside her burgundy Nissan Altima. She glanced at the picture of Tamil laid out on the couch fucked up, then her and Tamil sitting at the table with big cups of rum and Coke.

Joy had lived with Bugg for three months until she saved enough to get her a place. Tamil worked with her and had a passion for black men. She wasn't really accepted by white or black women, but for some reason, her being white never bothered Joy because she was cool, so they clicked.

When Tamil was going through it with her husband, she asked Joy for a place to stay. Joy knew how it felt not having a place to stay, and opened her door. Besides, the extra money was well needed, and what was meant to be a couple weeks turned to eight months.

Joy shook her head, reminiscing about the most experimental times of her life. Tamil made her open up. Living with her was like waking up and going to bed with adventure. Sadly, as days passed, she realized Tamil was going through a rough time as usual, always fussing with her husband, always stressed. Then she began to see Tamil spend most of her evenings drinking and on the computer.

One evening Tam sat with her rum and Coke and a big smile on her face, typing away at the computer. Joy came up beside her to see what she was doing and asked why she was smiling.

"This is some shit called Tagged that my husband best friend turned me on to. He knew my husband was fuckin' around on me and use to see me in the house crying and shit. Then one day we were just talking, and he told me I needed some friends."

"What? Your husband best friend told you that?"

"Yeah, he got a girl, but he ain't married or nothing. He said he got a lot of friends off this site that he talk to. He my friend too. He be sending me tags and shit too."

"Yeah. But why would he try and get his best friend wife to meet other guys? That don't sound right. Fuck it! That ain't my business. So what is it again?" Joy asked as she stood over Tamil's shoulder.

"It's a Web site that you go to and meet people," she said. "I'm talking to a guy now that's real cool."

"I can't meet a man on a computer. That shit seem desperate." Joy smirked.

"Naw, you just talk to them. I'll show you. You'll get a lot of friends."

Joy shook her head as she turned the page and looked at herself in the picture with Tamil, all the other friends she'd met during a very trying time in her life. Joy went from meeting guys online, to going out to meet them, to eventually inviting them over and spending time with them. And after a minute she was being pulled into swing parties. Later on, she realized it was a fuck site, somewhere you go and meet people to fuck.

It wasn't long before they were meeting dudes from all walks of life. Soon they were hanging out at some of the most exclusive parties. For the couple years of her life, she would have any fantasy or thought of sex that she gathered come to life. And in these years, she met some of the most desperate, scandalous, disgraceful men she'd ever come across.

She looked at the picture of Don standing in his briefs with his bony ass, looking like he was on crack, which he probably was. But Tamil showed her how enough liquor could make you not give a damn. He was the first dude she'd met online and allowed to come into her world. He came in the door treating her like candy, licking and tasting every part of her body, showing her body attention it had never been shown.

After a couple months, what started fast and exciting turned into this nigga having a family and Joy was just his getaway. So she stepped back. But he still came around from time to time. He became her friend.

Joy sat shaking her head as she looked at Tommy. Tears formed in her eyes as she thought about how, at that time, she was hurting so bad, she let Tamil introduce her to the brother of a guy she'd met. He was married but having problems and needed a friend. Joy was skeptical because she had just been hurt by finding out about Don, but she put it in her mind that since he'd told her up front, he was being fair. She allowed herself to let go and enjoy Tommy. And she did, but she soon got tired of the smoking, drinking, and him just coming at night fucking her silly then leaving.

She soon found out some valuable news from Tamil one Saturday morning when she came in from one of her all-nighters. Tamil came in the door as Joy sat at the computer on Tagged at six in the morning, looking grim, checking her messages.

"What up, girl?" Tamil asked.

"Nothing. Talking to Omari."

"Y'all been talking a minute, and you only met him once?"

"We went to lunch a couple times."

"And? You fuck him yet?" Tamil was smiling.

"Naw, I ain't doing that to Tommy," Joy said.

"You act like you and Tommy serious," Tamil said with a twisted face.

"He don't want me fucking nobody, and I know he chilling. He getting ready to leave his wife and get his own shit. The way that dude put it down, I know he ain't nowhere else," Joy said.

Tamil began to laugh. "Joy, you know men and how they wanna fuck, but you don't know men. First of all, I was with him and his wife Thursday. All of us went out. Tommy and his wife are doing fine. They just bought a new house. That's why he carried you to his old one and fucked you, talking about he getting his own, and she walking around here big as a house, pregnant.

"Damn, Tamil! Why he lie? Why he carrying it like I'm all that to him and I turn him on like nobody else? This shit hurts," Joy said, tears welling up in her eyes.

"Joy, men will say anything. I mean anything to get you open, not just to get the pussy, but so they can keep getting the pussy without the interruption of other guys. See, the reason you feel so good to Tommy is because it's wrong in his mind, so it turns him on. You are a trick. He thinks that, so it turns him on. He's sneaking around, in and out, treating you like shit for real, but taking you out, buying you shit, but in the long run, you are just a trick. When niggas cheat, it's a turn-on to them, but if you looking for love, then you gonna be hurt. You been fucking Tommy for five months and you open, but not in love. You vulnerable.

"I haven't said this because I don't want you to get mad, but you still love Minke. You trying to find a replacement, but you can't. You fuck, so you'll have friends, because you don't wanna be alone. Because if any man come up to you and say, 'I'm married, but I really like you and want some time,' he really saying, 'You look like a dumb bitch who head ain't on straight. And I want some of your time so I can convince you to allow me to come by so we can fuck whenever I can get away from my wife.'" Tamil was serious.

Joy smiled with a hurt heart. She was confused.

"I been out here a long time, Joy, and I found out most men got a woman. And if they don't, and you like him, go all out, but if they do, get 'em." Tamil smiled a wicked smile. "My shit is fun. You met Omari and like him. Tell him to come fuck the shit out of you, so you can forget the pain."

Tamil typed an instant message on the computer: *I'm lonely come spend the day making me feel better.*

"Fuck that shit! You don't belong to nobody," Tamil said seriously. "If you ain't gonna get no money out of these dudes, then you better truly enjoy the sex."

Sounds like a winner, but I'm at work. Get off at noon and I can come through with drinks and goodies.

Tamil typed: *Waitin' on you.*

They laughed and ran in the room to find Joy some sexy lounging wear.

Joy turned her head to the other page and smiled at the pictures of herself in big throw dresses. She reminisced about the day Omari came by and how that friendship started. She had told him everything about her, and he told her his life story. They shared so much, until Tommy showed up after she ignored his call most of the day.

After many bangs at the door, she finally answered.

"What the fuck you doing?" he yelled as he came in the door, pushing her. He noticed Omari on the couch.

Joy's heart dropped. She'd never been here.

"This is what you doing now? Fuckin' other niggas?"

"Tommy, this is my friend Omari. Omari, I told you about Tommy," Joy said softly as Omari stood to his feet. "I'm your friend, Tommy, not your woman. You are married."

"What the fuck you mean? My being married didn't mean shit when yo' big ass was lonely as hell, willing to do anything to keep my company. Fuck it! I got to find me another jump-off. I done fucked you every way possible anyway. Nasty, fat bitch! Now you picking random niggas, giving away pussy. But thanks. You made my relationship stronger, because every day I spent fucking you and letting you suck my dick, on the way home I stopped and bought my wife a gift, thanking her for not being like you hoes in the street." Tommy walked out, slamming the door.

Joy's heart was already in her stomach, but now it just churned. She felt low, embarrassed, and she knew Omari was out.

For Tommy to act like that, the head and pussy must be the bomb. "Are you okay?" Omari asked.

"Damn," she said softly. "I never thought—"

"Sometimes surprises aren't good. You should have picked up the phone and said something. Well, I guess now he knows you got a new man." Omari hugged her.

Joy felt like shit and really wanted him to leave. She called Tamil, who rushed straight home, knowing her friend was in a bad situation. Tamil came in, and they went to the room and talked. That's when she was introduced to the cocaine game. Tamil showed her a line of coke and a shot of alcohol could do wonders for the mind and body.

And later that night she allowed her mind to relax and let Omari do whatever he wanted to her body. And he did everything Minke, Bugg, Don, and Tommy did to perfection. Except, his ten-inch dick stretched her body to different heights. By morning she knew who had first dibs on her.

In months to come, after her feelings had escalated for Omari, his visits became less frequent, and even though she'd gone through it with Tommy, she let him back in the door. Now over a year had passed, and she still felt like nothing inside.

Joy remembered running into her old hairdresser, Lady Swann. Lady Swann ran Swann Terrace Boutique. Most of the hustler girls got their hair done at her shop. And by her saying she was from NY, it made all the New York girls go to her when they came to town. Joy remembered when she ran into Lady Swann.

She hadn't seen her since she'd lost her home when Minke cut her off. She couldn't think of going to Lady Swann's salon with no money, and the dudes she was fucking wasn't coming off nothing but dick.

"Oh my God! Joy!" Lady Swann yelled as they embraced. "Where the hell you been, girl?"

"Moving around, you know."

"This is me, girl. Don't play. You know I'm the realest bitch on Norfolk Street. Why you ain't come to see me?"

"I been fucked up, girl. Trying to keep afloat. You know that nigga had me fucked up."

"I know. I heard. And I don't knock niggas for how they act or what they do, because some bitches deserve it, but don't leave the kids fucked up," Lady said with an attitude.

"For real, girl, nigga had me out there."

"You eating good. Look at you. You got big as hell. Face still cute as ever," Lady said as Joy smiled.

"Yeah, I put on a little bit," Joy said sadly.

"Girl, lift your head up. Them big-ass titties and little waist and phat ass. If you put yourself together, you'll fuck niggas up, girl. Look, come by the shop tomorrow about noon."

"Got to work. Don't get off till five."

"Come afterwards. Come straight there. Don't be bullshitting, or I'm gonna leave ya fucked up," Lady said seriously.

"Thank you, for real."

Joy, knowing how she was, made sure she headed to Lady Swann's Boutique right after work.

Joy grabbed her bottle of Riesling and turned it over, pouring the last bit into her glass. "Better carry my ass to sleep before I can't get up in the morning," she said out loud.

She flipped some more pages and saw the pictures of her and Omari down the beach at the house in Sand-bridge. She began to smile, thinking about that time he'd invited to a party some of his friends were hav-ing. When she went and saw Lady Swann, she made sure to let her know, and Lady hooked her up with her fly-ass short cut she'd always had, applied her makeup perfectly, and told the nail tech, Romaine, who rented a spot in her shop, to look out on a manicure and pedi-cure. She left out of the salon, looking like a million bucks and floating on cloud nine.

When Omari showed up to pick her up, he stood at the door and stared at her in the short hot pink dress and matching sandals, the hot pink eye shadow caked up over her eyes. He was turned on and felt tonight was gonna be on point.

"Yo, you know your red nightie and robe that I like?"

"Yeah," she answered, confused.

"Go get it. We not coming back. You with me to-night," he said smiling.

As they made their way down to the beach, he pulled out a little pack of coke for them to get their head right. When they arrived, the party was in full swing. The women had on sexy outfits, all the men had on boxers or pajama pants, and the music was good. And as he moved around he explained the rules to her.

"This is a girl-girl room and no men are allowed. All the other rooms got different themes going on, and if you want to participate, just ask and go for it. After ev-ery episode, you need to shower and brush your teeth then get another drink." Omari smiled. "Oh, and if anybody try to run up in you raw, let it be known, and they'll throw them out."

"And suppose I'm kinda shy and not ready for this?" she asked, feeling funny, wishing he'd told her exactly what this was about. She stared at him and the things going on around her. "Tell me, Omari. Why would you bring me here? Seriously, I want to know."

Omari could tell at that moment she was uncomfortable. He stared at her. "I got to be honest with you, Joy. When we met online, I took you as a single mom with a lot to offer, and when I say a lot to offer, I mean time, attention, conversation, and possibly love. I wanted a woman in my life who had time for me and only me.

"Before you, I had broken up with my girl. We had a four-year relationship, but between her work and school, and her taking care of grandmother, that left little time for me. She was always good to me and always kept it one hundred, so when I felt she couldn't focus on me, I didn't play her. I left her ass and I told her why. Then I met you and spent my time online talking to you. So when we met, I was getting into you. Then your boy Tommy came through. That shit shook me, but it didn't change the way I felt. I just thought he was a jealous ex. But that same night he hurt you, you fucked me still like it really didn't faze you. Then many nights, your phone ring off the hook, twelve, one, two in the morning. That was too much. Dudes come to your house knocking all times of the night, and the kicker was, I went to one of these parties last month in D.C., and Tommy was there. He let me know he was still fucking you, and he asked me to ask you if we could fuck you together. I was really hurt, but played it off. Then he told me of your other friends, and it killed me. But I don't judge. I'm just looking for love and my own. This is fun, and that's what you are to me, nothing more. So, yes, I can do this with ya," he said, staring at her.

Joy's eyes welled up with tears. "I was married, and I want to be married again. I want love and respect, I don't want this. I was lonely, just me and my kids, and I don't want to be alone," she said softly as a tear dropped. She had allowed herself to catch feelings over Omari and didn't know what to do at that point.

"I'm always up front, Joy. I carried it like this because I felt it was all a game to you. And when I found out you was still dealing with these other dudes . . ." Omari began to smile.

"What's funny?"

"When dudes hurt, they do strange things. But, no matter what, we don't want to be alone. I thought I had found something real in you, but that nigga shut all that down for me. When he shut me down, I didn't want to deal with it by myself. So I"—Omari paused—"Don't take this the wrong way, but last month I went and bought a bracelet and a ring, took it to my girl, and begged her to take me back, thanking God she ain't like these nasty bitches in here," he said, looking around.

"Well, I'm not for this, and I don't get down like this. I would really like to leave."

"Well, I apologize. I'll take you home," he said, headed back downstairs.

When they arrived back at her home, Omari walked her inside and had a drink. She never said a word on the ride home or since they'd gotten in the house.

He walked to the door and turned to her. "Sorry again, Joy. I guess I took you wrong. Hope we still cool. I definitely enjoy your company. I'ma call you. Oh! And let me put a bug in your ear about Tommy—he go both ways. He done a lot of time locked up, and he just wanna get a nut, he don't care how. So I hope you use condoms with any dude you with. Be careful," he said and left out.

Joy stood there with her mouth open and mind confused. At that moment she felt she never wanted to be with another guy again. *How could I trust them?*

Tamil came out as Joy was sitting down, crying, thinking about how it came that Omari thought she was like those other trifling girls at that party and that she wanted to swing. She sat beside her and gave her a drink.

Joy listened to Tamil as she tried to console her, until they sat embraced in each other's arms crying. Tamil told her to put on the red, sexy outfit, so she could feel pretty and look like the extraordinary woman she knew she was, that maybe she needed a reminder.

They sniffed and took a couple drinks, and Joy went and changed. When she returned, they sniffed some more and did some shots. Joy was still feeling down. She just wanted to go to bed. Tamil walked her in her room, and they climbed in bed.

Joy frowned as she thought about the time in her life that she was lost. But she smiled as she turned the page. A burst of energy came through her body, and tears came to her eyes. She drank her last bit of wine and closed the photo album and held it to her chest. The tears fell as she cried, but they weren't tears of pain, but tears of relief and joy.

She flashed back to the night of humiliation, desperation, and torture. She turned off her light and laid back still holding her photo album, as that Saturday night played in her head. But the worst was when she woke up 6:34 A.M. that Sunday morning in Tamil's bed.

Joy looked over at Tamil laid back, fucked up, and naked, her legs wide open. She shook her head, not believing her life, not believing herself, and began to wish she was dead.

She sat up on the side of the bed, glanced over at the nightstand, at the large black dildo and massager. Disgust went through her body. She got up and went to get her clothes and saw the used condoms on the floor. She knew Tam had either fucked before she came home, or last night, or while she was 'sleep in the bed right next to her. Her heart hurt, her self-esteem was shot.

She looked in at her kids then walked into the bathroom and got the Tylenol with codeine. Her head was banging so hard, and her body shook. She couldn't stop the tears from flowing down her face. She wanted the pain to stop. She wanted the thoughts of Minke not wanting her to stop.

She tilted the bottle to take two of the 800 milligram pills, but a handful fell out as thoughts of her grandmother she'd lost years ago came into her mind. She smiled and lifted the pills to her mouth.

Just then, she heard her phone ring. She wanted to ignore it, but it wouldn't stop. "Gotdamn! Can I die?" she yelled as she threw the pills in the toilet and stormed back in the bedroom. "What?" she answered, not recognizing the number.

"You all right?" Lady said. "I love you, Joy."

"What you mean? Why you say that?"

"I don't know. I was up, getting ready for church, and God told me to call you, let you know you are loved, that I care, and He will always be there, and that's the only love you need in your life. Come to church with me, girl. Service start at eight thirty. Get dressed and come, bring your kids, wear whatever. This church is like that," Lady said sincerely, not knowing why she was doing this.

"Yes, Lady. Yes. I'll come. Me and these kids are coming. Where?" Joy was crying, thinking about what had almost happened.

"What's wrong, Joy?"

"I promise I'll talk to you when I see ya."

"Okay, we'll go to my house after the service. I'm cooking. The church is on Holland Road. City of Refuge."

"See ya, Lady, and thanks. Leave your phone on in case I get lost, but I'm coming."

Joy got her kids up, and they all got dressed and went to church. Once Joy entered, she felt something within the walls that couldn't be explained. As she sat next to Lady and praised, she talked to God until tears ran down her face like a fountain.

The bishop saw her face, looked over at Lady, as the church calmed and everyone sat. He started off by saying he had studied a sermon all week and had it ready for delivery, but today God brought something else to his heart. He began to speak on "Adultery and the Weakness of the Flesh."

Joy felt as if he was talking directly to her the entire sermon, and every word cut her like the swords they had become.

And as the bishop opened up the doors of the church, Joy slowly moved her tortured body down the narrow aisle until she reached the pulpit.

The bishop came down and took both her hands and leaned closer. "Have you accepted God into your life, young lady?" he asked in a strong voice.

"No," she said softly.

"Have you taken the time to ask for forgiveness?"

"I—I—I don't know how," Joy said in a stutter.

"Look at me, sister. It's time," he said, squeezing her hand. "It's time. It's time to grab God's hand. It's time to let go and let God, sister."

Joy's body shook as the bishop held her hand.

"Now repeat after me," he said. "Dear Heavenly Father, I come to you as humble as I know how, asking Your forgiveness. For I am repenting and asking You because only You can help me for all the sins that I've committed. And from this day forward, I will only be led by the light that shines in me through You."

"Now from this day forward, sister, allowing God to be your guide, let the church be your strength, and I promise you will come out of whatever weighs you down. For we can do all things through Christ, who strengthens us." Bishop stared into her eyes as he held her hand.

Joy stood tall, and the tears began to dry up. She felt strength in her body that she hadn't felt in a long time. She felt as if she had been born again and given a new life.

After church, she went over to Lady's house, where her kids played with Lady's kids.

Lady had five kids by five different men. Her life was wild at one time, but she changed it three years ago for the better and always, no matter what, gave the glory to God. She sat in the kitchen cooking and telling Joy how God had changed her life.

As they sipped wine, Joy had to talk to someone, and she opened up to Lady and told her everything. How she was living, fucking all the men, and laying with funny women.

When Joy was finished, Lady looked her in the eyes, took her hand, and told her, "Girl, you just told me the PG version of my life. You have no idea. But guess what? You are a new woman now, born again, and the first thing you gonna do is get that devil out your house. Tell all those guys you done with them and you got saved today. Stop being there for them to use, and stop fucking them. The ones that stick around for nothing will show you who's your friend. Now chill out, eat, be merry, and prepare yourself to clean house. Clean your house," Lady said, smiling.

Joy went home that Sunday evening and had a long talk with Tamil. Joy gave her a week to get her shit straight and make a move, but later that night Tamil was gone.

"Thank you, Jesus," Joy said loudly, shaking her head as she climbed under the covers, thinking about how she had made drastic changes that all worked for the better.

Over the next several months, she was only available to Don, Tommy, Bugg, and Omari for conversation. She kept herself close to Lady, her head into the Bible studying, never missing church or Bible study. Slowly but surely she moved away from the life that made her feel low and made sure she didn't let anyone in to break her spirits.

Everybody stopped calling her when she changed the conversation to God every time they brought up sex. All but Omari, who continued to call, always had conversation, and always asked for sex. Several months had passed, and the only man in her life was God.

Omari popped up one Friday evening at the door right after she had come in from a prayer meeting.

"What you want, boy?" Joy asked surprised and smiling. She had been going to church faithfully, just like work. The rest of her time was focused on her kids, so she left no time for nonsense. Happy to see him, she gave him the biggest hug, and he squeezed her back, holding her a little longer than expected.

"Damn, I forgot how cuddly your little short, fat ass was. Come here." He smiled and grabbed her again.

Then he stepped back and looked at her. "You look good as hell. For real, Joy, you look good," he said, amazed.

"Thanks. Fat and all, huh!"

"Please. You been turning me on forever, and I love it. Now you gonna make a nigga go to church and get some of that pussy," he said, laughing.

Joy laughed too. She knew out of all her old friends, he always kept shit one hundred. And that wasn't going to change. Omari was always himself.

"So what you doing here?"

"Got this Tyler Perry bootleg. Throw it in. Cook something, and I'm chilling for a little bit." Omari sat down and grabbed her remote, making himself at home. "Hand me a glass," he said, popping the top of his twenty-two-ounce Heineken.

She handed him the glass and walked to her room. She returned in her sweats and t-shirt to a room, filled with the sweet smell of Kush. She stopped in her tracks and stared at him.

"Fuck I suppose to do? Go outside? Come on, Joy."

She shook her head and walked in the kitchen. She poured a glass of wine and began dinner.

As the night progressed and the movie ended, she found out that evening that no matter how much she read the Bible, went to church, and tried to put God first, the flesh was weak. And Omari became her weakness.

But this time, in her eyes and heart, it was different. She wasn't running a mile a minute, and her head wasn't in a whirlwind. For once in her life she felt in control, but she wanted Omari to herself. She wouldn't feel it was wrong if she felt he was her man.

"Where you trying to take this, Omari? Who you dealing with? Where your girl?"

"I have a friend, but we don't spend a lot of time. She work hard, and she on some real come-up shit. It's like she there, but she not. She got her own shit, but I stay at home. All my shit at my momma house," he said, laughing.

Joy laughed along also.

"I know I feel good with you," Omari said. "And I know I enjoy you, and I miss you. I don't fuck with that sex shit no more, and I haven't been on Tagged in a long time. It came to disgust me. I knew it was wrong, but I was on some other shit. Now, here is where I want to be."

Looking in her eyes, Omari realized that's what she wanted to hear, and she melted into his arms. Right away, he began kissing, squeezing, and touching her in those spots he already knew would excite her, until she gladly gave in.

Afterwards he held her tight and fell asleep, and she smiled a different smile that night.

Over the next several weeks, Omari showed interest like never before. If he didn't stay overnight, they'd talk every day, and whenever her phone rang and she saw his number, a feeling of joy took over her body and she could do nothing but smile.

Joy never knew exactly what changed his outlook and why he began to cling to her as if she was his woman, but it made her feel good, and she devoured every bit of attention he had to give, and he gave it willingly.

As time progressed though, Joy began to outgrow Omari. She wanted more, for her kids, for herself. Whenever, she brought it up to him, he clearly let her know he was happy with their current situation, coming and going as he pleased, staying a couple nights a week.

Yes, he cared for her, and yes, he enjoyed her, and yes, her kids were not a problem to him. But moving out of his moms and in with her meant being a family, and the last thing he wanted was a ready-made family.

Even though they'd been together a second and she loved him in every way, Joy was starting to come at him strong, and that eventually slowed him down from coming around. She was bothered in the beginning because she'd gotten used to his company and his daily phone calls, but now she realized she had church and a good friend in Lady.

CHAPTER 6

Joy remembered when her phone rang Wednesday morning. They had talked till the late hours so the call wasn't unexpected.

"Hey, Joy, my friend left me a message last night while we were on the phone. He a longshoreman, and they having a party at the Longshoreman Hall Saturday. I want you to go with me and a couple other girls I know," Lady said.

"Girl, I heard it ain't nothing but old-ass men in there." Joy wondered why she wanted to go there. Then she thought about Lady's age. She was about thirty-eight, so maybe that was her bag.

"Joy, not old men, older mature men. I'm gonna show you how to come up. Get out from under the strain and keep doing what you doing," Lady Swann said real calm. "Let you see where the Swann come from, girl." She chuckled.

"I'm only twenty-eight, and those niggas ain't got shit I want."

"Just flow with me. I want you to swing. Let's go shopping, and I got you Saturday morning, your hair on me. You gonna be the flyest bitch. Lord forgive me, but that's what it's gonna be," Lady Swann said with a smirk. "Promise you, you'll enjoy yourself."

"I'm with it. That, or sit in the house waiting on O."

"That's your fix, girl. He gonna always be your friend, but you need security and to be shown that attention that only comes with a mature nigga on a mission."

"Uugh! Huh! I'm gonna go to the mall and see what I see."

"Naw, come by the shop this evening. I got something for ya. For real, come by, all right?"

"Gotcha. One!" Joy hung up.

Saturday came, and everybody met at Lady's house to get dressed and got their head right before going to the party. When Joy walked out of the room, the other girls were like, "Damn!"

"Lady, you did it again. Walk, girl," Daria said, talking to Joy. Daria was one of the stylists in the Swann House Beauty Salon.

Joy strutted across the floor and looked at the other women and turned. She then turned to Lady and smiled.

"How you feel, baby girl?" Lady asked.

"Like a lady." Joy smiled. "Thank you, Lady. Feel like a new me," she added.

"Her hair is fizzed, girl. You are definitely a banger," one of the other stylists said.

"Yeah, now I just need to lose forty to fifty pounds and I'll really be in there," Joy said with a smirk.

"Girl, you gonna find out that men love a voluptuous bitch. It's just something about us," Lady's sister said, squeezing her forty-GG's together. "I ain't been alone in years, and I got me a husband, so fuck these skinny bitches."

They all laughed.

Part of Joy's depression and insecurity came from her being overweight. She knew back in the day, these cornball-ass niggas she'd allowed to enter into her world would have never got in, but life had thrown some shit in the game.

They all headed out the door, and Joy jumped in the truck with Lady.

When they arrived at the Longshoremen's Hall, Joy strolled in stepping hard in her open-toe canary yellow sandals with the three-inch heels that flowed perfectly with the strapless denim dress that buttoned down the front. She'd purposely left the bottom three buttons loose, exposing her thighs. And her back and shoulders were exposed, leaving onlookers wondering if her breasts and the rest of her body were as smooth.

They came in and found their seats at a table and pulled out their bottles. Joy had never been to a BYOB, but as they got into the night, she actually began to enjoy herself. She was eating up the attention that was coming her way by the gentlemen at the party, and dying off the older men dressed in colorful suits and shoes like they were pimping. Some even had the hats to match.

They laughed, joked, and drank. Some even threw in a dance or two. Everybody was dancing, while Joy sat at the table watching Lady work moves on her friend who invited her to the dance. She saw this guy who looked so familiar approaching their table, but she couldn't place the face, until he got right up on her.

"Alecia," he asked, pointing, a big question mark on his face.

"Yeah." she said smiling, knowing she knew this guy, but didn't remember from where.

"Praize, baby. You remember me?" He acted as if he was going to pop-lock, and they both burst out laughing.

"What's up? How are you?" Joy didn't run into or remember many people from school because she wasn't that social when she moved from NY. Soon after she'd met Minke, and it was all about him.

"I'm doing good. And you?"

She stood up and gave him a hug. He sat down for a few and caught up, exchanged numbers, and made his exit. She realized after he talked with her, he was out the door. No sooner than he left, she looked up, and Daria was sitting back down with two older gentlemen. Daria kept them both entertained as Joy looked on.

"So, who are you, miss? Over here like she ain't never been to a longshoreman dance. Like she don't know what it is, Ben," the loud man yelled, giving his partner a high-five.

"Leave her alone, Finn. You might scare her. Is she scared, darling?" Ben asked Daria.

"Hell naw. She ain't scared. She chillin', getting her sexy on. Get her, Finn." Daria smiled at Joy.

Joy looked back at her and laughed. All night long these older cats had been on it. She'd seen them move around, talk to women, get turned down, and before the girl could finish saying no, they turned to the next woman. For a sec, she wished Praize hadn't left. At least he had decent conversation.

"So what's your name, darling?" Finn yelled over the music.

Standing six foot one, drink in his hand, with his clean-shaven face, and looking in shape for the age his face read, he wasn't bad too Joy, but he looked too old, and he had a big round belly. "Alecia. And how are you? Finn, right?" she asked with a smile, determined to have a good time.

"Damn! You's a sexy woman," Finn said, throwing both hands up and doing a dance.

"Thank you."

"So how you living, young lady?" Finn asked as he sat down in the chair behind Joy.

"What you mean?" she asked, confused by the question.

"That's a one-'n'-all question, baby—Do you got a man? Do you have a family? Do you work? How you surviving? Good, bad, getting by? Maybe I should have said, how you living?" Finn said seriously, in a lower tone, moving closer to Joy.

Joy thought his cologne was something she'd smelled before on her momma's friends.

She looked at Finn. "No, I'm single, just friends, got two kids, and I'm surviving with the help of God, the only real man in my life. And you?" Her direct response and eye contact made her come off strong.

"Well, I'm married for thirty years. Done raised three young'uns, and now I enjoy life in every way. I need a young thing like you in my life," he said, looking her up and down. I'm sixty-five. Don't got time for the games, but I like ya."

"You a longshoreman?"

"No, I'm into real estate," he said, handing her his card. "I used to be a longshoreman."

"Call me tomorrow. Promise you will, if nothing else."

"I will," she responded, figuring he was a nice old man.

By this time, Lady came back to the table with three men on her. Lady wore a black catsuit, with one arm and shoulder exposed. Her strapless bra did a lot for her breasts—she didn't have much—but they sat as if they were just about to pop out, but never did, but her large nipples that stayed hard, and showed, had those men drooling.

Finn and Ben said their good-byes, while everyone else took seats.

"This is Vince, Lopez, and Wendell," Lady said, introducing them to Daria and Joy.

"Hello." Joy spoke to all, but admired the youngest of the three.

Lopez shook her hand. He reminded her of the Puerto Rican kids she'd grown up with in New York. He was real light, almost white, but his accent let you know.

They began talking, until her phone began to ring. It was Omari. Joy really wanted to see him, but she was having fun meeting new people, getting numbers, and her mind was free.

"What up?" she answered.

"Where you at?"

"Told you I was coming to a party tonight," she said.

"I know. I'm outside. Come on, it's after one."

"I'm riding with Lady. I'll meet—"

"No, I'll take you to your car. Come on now. I want to see you. Now! I'm out front," he said and hung up.

Joy looked at Lopez. For some reason she was attracted to this guy. He was cool, laid-back.

"Yo, Lady, I'm out. My ride's out front. I'm gonna call you later." She stood and hugged her. "It was nice meeting you all, and I'm sure I'll see you again," she said, stepping off.

Lopez was right behind her, on her heels. "Excuse me, but can I get your number? I see you in a hurry to leave, but there's some things I'd like to discuss with you." He smiled.

"And what's that, Mr. Lopez?"

"Me and you," he said, staring back into her eyes.

"Two, nine, seven . . ." she said and eased out the door.

Sitting right in front, where she couldn't miss him, was Omari. He glimpsed at her and did a double take, locking his eyes on her every move as she strutted to his car.

"What up, baby?" she asked, getting in the car.

He just stared at her and smiled, not saying anything.

"You acting crazy, boy. Come on and go."

Omari pulled off, shaking his head. Joy didn't know what he was thinking.

"What's with all this here?" he finally asked, waving his hand up and down at her, from head to toe.

"I just wanted to put myself together a little more."

"What you mean? You cute as shit. You don't need all that. Where that come from?"

"I don't know. Lady hooked it up. She said I would feel better, and I do. You don't like it?" she asked, disappointed.

"Just curious about when you started revealing all that skin and wearing all that shit. That's not you," he said, pulling up to her car. "I'm following you."

She got out the car and stumbled.

"You that fucked up? You a alcoholic now too?" he said as she shut the door. He began laughing.

As she drove home, her phone rang. It was Lopez wanting to know if he could come by. She actually wanted to talk with him, so she didn't say no. She told him she would give him a call when she got settled.

When she arrived, she found her kids knocked out and the sitter half 'sleep. She paid her and watched her walk across to the next building.

"Get us a beer," Omari said as he walked into her room and sat on the bed. He heard her locking up and getting beers as he rolled a Backwood.

"Damn!" she yelled as she handed him the beer. "That shit smell good as hell. What is it?"

"Kush. Ain't but the truth," he said between pulls. He handed it to her, knowing she had stopped.

"I'm good."

"Naw, we smoking, celebrating all this new sexiness," he said, pulling her to him and pushing the Kush in her hand.

She stood smoking in front of him as he began to unbutton her dress. It opened and fell to the floor. He couldn't do nothing but stare.

She began to cover her big stomach with her hands and arms. "You know I don't want nobody to see all this," she said conscious of her body, mainly her belly that lapped over the thong that you could barely see.

He took the Back and hit it, reached over and grabbed the remote and turned to the hip-hop station. Then he reached out and pushed her hands and arms away from her stomach.

"Step back and turn around," he said, and she did. He looked at her rolls on her side, but he also caught the flawless caramel skin that made him want to lick her plus-size body. He wanted his tongue to follow the thong in the crack of her ass.

"Look at me. Turn around."

She did.

He stared into her eyes, which had been lined with dark eyeliner, making them appear chinky. Her extended eyelashes made him feel as if her eyes were caressing him, and her smooth skin that rose on her cheekbones every time she blushed and the lips that covered her beautiful white teeth made him want to throw his tongue in her mouth.

"Move. Dance. Just move to the music," he said standing up reaching out for her, as she came close, dancing to the music.

He put both his hands on the outside of her breasts and pushed them together. As they rose up in the strapless canary yellow bra, he could feel his manhood rise then stiffen in his True Religion jeans. He reached behind her, undid her bra, and brought each end around to the front. Omari watched those 42DD's slide out of their secure sling and rest on her stomach. He took his hands and grabbed one, throwing one of her nipples into his mouth and licking and sucking vigorously.

She reached out and took off his Polo and his T-shirt in one swoop. Before his shirt could hit the floor, he was behind her, pushing her to the bed.

Joy leaned over on the bed, thinking he was gonna drop his pants like he'd done lately and just push his manhood up into her, but he fell to his knees and allowed his tongue to follow her thong into her ass and between her legs. He pulled the thong to the side and buried his face into her warm, moist womanhood from behind, and sucked and devoured, until he found her clit and licked and flickered as he spread her ass.

Joy spread her legs, so he would have no problems getting to what was eventually going to make her body feel more than sensational, and it did. She lifted her ass and opened her legs as far as they would go, allowing him all access. Then a feeling rose from her insides, and she let out a scream.

A gush of warmth ran down Omari's nose and onto his top lip and in his mouth. He never stopped indulging, until she closed her legs and lunged forward, not being able to take another lick.

Joy heard his buckle loosen and his pants drop. When he approached the bed and touched her, she was still shaking, going through a moment of ecstasy, and didn't want anything to disturb it. So she turned sideways and came to the edge of the bed and reached out and grabbed his erection and took it into her mouth.

She could feel his excitement by the stiffness of his penis and the way it jerked at her touch.

Omari leaned back, breathing hard.

As she got into her rhythm, her body relaxed, and she became even more excited, knowing what she was doing for him.

Joy got on her knees facing him, never removing his dick from her mouth. She stuck her ass up high in the air, so he could imagine getting in it, as she sucked him off. Her tongue and head motion coming together, she could feel his dick swelling.

Omari began to pant hard. "I'm gonna cum," he said, giving her the option, but she never pulled back.

He felt a feeling of ecstasy begin to rise up inside of him as her tongue flickered across the underside of his dick, right below the head.

He let out an, "Aaagh!" that could have woke the kids. He thought the feeling was going to be interrupted, but it wasn't, as he stood shaking, releasing every bit of cum into her mouth.

Joy squeezed and sucked until he pushed her head back and fell to his knees, and then flat on his back, trying to catch his breath.

"Whoa!" he said, getting to his feet, his dick in his hand. He stared at the bashful fat girl laid back on the bed, legs open, head to the side, knocked out.

As soon as he climbed on top of her, she lifted her legs and allowed him to enter, and he laid his body against her soft, cushiony body, knowing there was no greater feeling.

As he held her in his arms, pumping in and out of her womanly love until that feeling came again, his body tensed, and she tightened her muscles, as if cutting off her pee, creating that snug fit on his penis. Right then Omari another load his love juice into her and collapsed on top of her.

Joy held him close and squeezed him. She knew she loved him, but she wanted and needed more.

He knew he loved her, and she was all that he needed, but he couldn't commit. He knew as long as he gave her time, more time, and more dick, he could keep things his way.

They woke the next morning in each other's arms, continuing from the night before. By ten o'clock, he was headed God knows where, while her and her kids headed to church.

By the time she got home from church and made her dinner, she'd gotten two calls from Lopez and three from Finn.

"Damn! You give an old head your number, they gonna call," she said, talking to Lady on the phone.

"Yeah! I meant to tell ya. Take numbers because them niggas will worry the shit out ya." Lady laughed.

"So what's with the dude Lopez? He seemed down-to-earth."

"Know what? He real cool, but it's something about him. I can't put my finger on it, but he fuck with a well-known dude name Donnie, and some half-ass hustler name Reese. Donnie, they say, fuck with that shit, and Reese, he stay locked so much, they don't know if he straight or gay."

"For real, should I even be talking to him?" Joy asked.

"Girl, like I say, I don't know. Just be careful."

"Speak of the devil," Joy said laughing. "He beeping in. Let me get this."

"Holla back."

Joy clicked over. "Hello."

"What up? I done called you several times. Thought I was gonna hear from you last night."

"Just got tied up. So what's up with you, Mr. Lopez?"

"You, ma. I was seriously feeling you last night. I don't want a thing from you, except your time. I want to stop by and see ya. What you drink?"

"Wine, preferably something sweet. I'm not a real drinker. That's not really my thing," she said, moving around her kitchen.

"You were doing your thing last night."

"And? I do what I want, when I want. I'm grown, but again, I said that's not my thing."

"Okay, ma, you smoke?" he asked, feeling her out.

"Sometimes."

"Well, I'm trying to see ya. Where you at?"

"Home."

"And where is home?"

"Norfolk, Ocean View."

"See ya. I'm on the way."

An hour later Lopez was calling for directions to Joy's apartment. She had called Omari to see where he was, since the last thing she wanted was to deal with some bullshit for nothing, over a guy she barely knew. She didn't figure he was coming by anyway, after the way he fucked last night. That hadn't happened in a while, coming two days in a row.

Lopez came by with wine and weed, and they sat talking from 8 P.M. to almost twelve, and she actually enjoyed his company.

As the days passed he came around more and more, never asking for or pursuing anything. He just wanted to be a friend. She wanted his weed and his time, but trying to maneuver around Omari was difficult. He had proven to be a true friend, and she didn't want to lose him.

After a couple months, she had to move and was short on cash. Omari was ghost when she needed him, but Lopez was right there to offer a helping hand, not just to loan money, but to be a roommate and offer a helping hand for a few months. She knew how things had worked out with Tamil and how things got easier, so it was worth the chance. So when she moved in her new place, Lopez was right there. He got new furniture for the apartment on credit, and he bought a new bedroom set for them, putting out a nice sum of money to make sure they were comfortable.

When they went to pick up his things from his man Donnie's house where he was staying, Joy realized the place was a familiar scene as she pulled up to the old row house. She walked inside as he ran upstairs.

"Give me a minute. These are my folks, Donnie, Reese, the rest of the team," he said laughing.

Donnie ran upstairs with Lopez as she sat down talking to Reese, who didn't have much to say, but just looked at her as if he was disgusted with her. Then they returned with a funny smell about them. Donnie walked Reese outside as Lopez came down the stairs with one bag holding all his clothes.

As they burst out headed back to the apartment, Joy tried to get the picture of the crackhouse out of her mind, but that wasn't possible. She knew she didn't give up Omari for this. She hadn't talked to him this last week, he hadn't called, so she never let him know she was moving.

It was Friday night, and they sat in the apartment sipping wine and smoking. It would be the first night she would share her bed with Lopez, and her last. She showered and put on her throw dress, one of her many dresses that she pulled over her head over her shoulders and which fit like a halter top. But the dress fell long, so if she wanted to make love, all she had to do was pull it up to give him some pussy and pull the top down to expose her breasts and allow the dress to wrap around her stomach and not expose what she was self-conscious about.

She came out the bathroom and climbed in bed. He had Dutches rolled. After they smoked, he undressed and climbed in bed. She frowned at him, thinking about his dirty body on her clean, new sheets.

Before Joy knew it, Lopez was on her, trying to throw his tongue in her mouth. His breath was foul, and he smelled funny, not fresh. She kissed his neck, and the nasty, salty taste almost made her gag, but he'd already slipped out his drawers and was putting himself inside her.

Dreading the encounter, she barely opened her legs, but he was already pumping and grabbing at her breasts. Though he was inside her, she could barely feel him. She maneuvered herself and tried to get him deeper, but it was no use.

Lopez pumped until he was dripping sweat, and as he began to cum, his body shook, his mouth fell open, and drool fell from his bottom lip onto her face, along with his sweat.

Joy turned to her side and closed her eyes to keep from cringing. She kept asking herself, *What have I done? What did I get myself into?*

Throughout the night, she felt his hands all on her, grabbing her breasts, squeezing her nipples, trying to ease inside her.

The following morning, she was awaken by his moving around early, not soon enough for her. Then he asked her to drop him at Donnie's house. She was mad, but at the same time, she jumped up and did it.

She watched him throw on drawers from out his bag, dirty jeans, and a dingy tee, never brushing his teeth or washing his face. She was livid.

When she got home, she decided to make her kids breakfast. She heard her phone ring, but she ignored it thinking it was Lopez. When the phone rang again, she went to pick it up. It was Omari.

"Hello," she answered, not really knowing what to say, all types of emotion running through her.

"Hello hell!" he yelled. "You move and don't say shit?"

"You haven't called, and I haven't heard from you."

"My pops passed away in D.C. My family been up there handling his affairs. He never divorced my mom, so it all fell in her hands. So what the fuck? I've been ghost for weeks at a time. You still call and let me know what's popping. Come on, Joy, don't fucking play me, son. What's up? Where you move to?"

"Little Creek Road," she said slowly.

"With a nigga?" he asked, hoping and praying she'd say no.

"Omari, he just a roommate. He helped me out. It's not like that. Please don't be mad," she said, ready to cry.

"Back to your old shit. Fuck you!" he said.

"No, Omari, please, I need to talk to ya. Come over, please," she cried.

"If your dude come home, I'm gonna lay him down. It's not a game, Joy."

"Come over now, please," she said.

Joy gave him the address and ran in her room to clean up. As she made her bed, she found Lopez's underwear wrapped in the sheets. When she held them up and saw the stains in his briefs that looked as if they'd been trampled on, she almost threw up. She straightened up by the time Omari arrived.

"What up, girl?" Omari asked as he walked in.

She saw him adjust his waist and knew he was prepared for the bullshit.

"So what the fuck you gonna do?"

She couldn't even look at him. She reached for the half-smoked Dutch in the ashtray and lit it. She hit it two times.

Omari looked at her strangely. "What the fuck! You on crack now?"

"Now you being stupid, Omari," she said seriously.

"Bitch, I will slap the shit out your fat ass!" he screamed. "You don't smell that shit? That don't smell like the weed we smoke. That's a woolah. That shit laced with crack. I know you ain't that stupid, Joy. Please tell me you knew that."

"No, I didn't. I just ain't think nobody would do that."

"Either you too naïve, or you just stupid, but either way, I can't get caught up in your shit," he said, heading out the door.

Joy called Omari about twenty times, but he never answered.

By the time Lopez returned back to the house Tuesday, she had moved her kids in her room and put his things in theirs. She let him know that because of the money he put up and all he'd done, she would allow him to stay for the month, but that was it.

For the next month, Joy called Omari nonstop and stayed on the phone with him for hours, especially when she was home, letting him know she wasn't fucking with Lopez. But Omari, being far from stupid, had a hard time with it.

Over the next several months, Omari became even more distant. He had actually begun to allow his feelings to get much deeper for Joy. Ever since that night of extreme passion, she had done something. The way she came across was what he wanted. She had impressed him.

He wasn't staying away by choice. Things in his life had changed, and he had things to bring together. But now he felt she was back to her games, and he wasn't about that. So he limited his time with her, to keep his feelings under control.

But Joy took it another way. At this point in her life she cared for him more than anyone, but she wasn't going to sit still and wait on anyone. She also realized she had to slow down because her encounters with men were getting ridiculous. The one with Lopez one she could have gone without.

And the thought of giving Finn her time was scary. She thought of the time she'd spent with him. Figuring he was married and older, she thought he would go by her rules and she could play him. She would lead, and the old man would follow.

She thought of the evening he called as she sat looking at *The First 48*.

It was about two months after Lopez had moved out when she ran into Reese at the new club on Baker Road, Luxury Brown. It was her and her old friend Malaina. Malaina actually made her feel good because she was the only friend she had that let herself go and got extra big. Malaina had married Wiz, had three kids, and blew up to a size eighteen.

When they stepped in the club that Wednesday evening for happy hour, they were dressed to impress, meaning, they both had on low-cut shirts, showing off their most important asset.

Joy, standing at five foot two, had her forty-two-DD's sitting out for attention, but Malaina shut her down as she strutted her five foot six frame across the floor. All men saw was the forty-four-GG breasts, small waist, big ass, and the long, black silky hair from the Filipino side of her family. She always thought she was the shit.

As her and Joy sat drinking on the Hennessy and Coke they ordered, Reese along with his boys, Stink, Cuz, Ray, and Fat Boy came up and surrounded them.

"So what up, ladies?" Reese said

"Hello. How are you?" Joy looked around to see if she saw his friend Lopez. "Where your man?"

"These my peoples," he said, introducing his boys.

"That nigga is a customer. I don't fuck with them like that. I was wondering how he pulled your ass." Reese smiled.

"He didn't pull me, he fooled me," she said seriously.

"She used to fuck with Lopez?" Ray asked Reese laughing. "He'll fool 'em all. Pretty Puerto Rican crackhead."

They all started laughing.

"It wa'n't like that. We were just cool." Joy was trying to save face. "Doing all that talking. Who got this next round?"

"I got you, whatever you want, Joy," Reese said, looking into her face.

Joy smiled at him. "Is that right?"

"And I got you," Fat Boy said. "What's your name?"

"Malaina."

"Malaina, I love you," Fat Boy said, staring at her breasts. "I'd give you anything. I just want you to hold me. Let me lay in your arms and hold me," he said seriously, leaning over and laying his head on her chest. "Wake me up in a hour," he said, laughing and raising up.

Drinks were ordered, and by the time happy hour ended, they all were feeling nice. Reese suggested they go smoke. The girls were down, so they all left out. She didn't know Reese and Fat Boy didn't have a car nor their own place.

"I'm riding with you, baby," Fat Boy said, putting his arm around Malaina.

She moved quickly. "No, ride with Joy. I got a man and don't know who out here. Who house we going to anyway?"

"We going to Joy house." Reese knew she stayed by herself, from what Lopez had told him.

"Why my house?"

"Because everybody got somebody at their house except you," Fat Boy said. "Your house is it."

"Who at your house, Reese?" Joy asked curiously.

"Wifey and four kids, mom, dad, brother. Shit! A houseful. Do it make a difference?" Reese stepped close to her. He didn't give a fuck if she was down or not. His man had already fucked her; he just wanted to play.

"Shit! We just going to smoke. What difference it make?" Fat Boy said.

They climbed in Joy's car and made their way to her apartment, Malaina following.

After three Dutches and many laughs from Fat Boy, everybody was comfy, but Malaina had to go, so she dropped Fat Boy off.

Reese made himself comfortable and chilled with Joy. They did a lot of talking that night, and over the next several days, and within two weeks, Reese was fucking the shit out her ass, whenever he could get away.

And he had talked her into allowing him to hold his drugs in her house, since he was spending so much time there. He was tired of running home to get his stash.

But his real reason was, he didn't like holding that shit around his family. He hit her off with weed and a couple dollars. She was an easy trick to him.

But her eyes were wide open. She really enjoyed his company. She was tired of being alone. He was around quite a bit, and by him having a wife, she could still feel free to do her thing. But over the next several months, his feelings got involved, and she was there for him whenever he wanted her. She even gave him a key.

Joy was happy with the situation. Being lonely was a thing of the past. She always had company now, since it had become his spot; coming in and find Fat Boy, Ray, Cuz, or any of his other friends there, bagging drugs, playing cee-lo, or having an intense poker game wa'n't shit.

It wasn't until Reese hadn't came around in a few days, though, that Omari stopped by and spent the night.

Reese came in about 2:30 A.M. after being dropped off and walked in the room to see her and Omari dead to the world, after a long, hard sex session. They never knew he had come in. He was getting ready to trip, but realized he couldn't get in trouble behind her. He had a wife, and fucking up his home was not happening.

Reese really began to slow his roll being over there, but a week later he walked in and found her laying across her bed crying, the house in disarray.

Believing he was truly a friend to her, she began to tell him about Finn, an older gentleman she'd met and was gonna try and get money out of. He had stopped by with a bottle, and she had showered and had on one of her throw dresses. As the drinks got going, Finn got more aggressive. She tried to calm the situation, but he got forceful and pulled her in her room. She didn't realize how strong the old man was until he put his arms around her and picked her up, palming her ass and falling on the bed.

Finn realized she wore no drawers under the long dress. He pulled it down, releasing her large breasts, and buried his head in them. She tried to struggle, but the old head was too strong. Before she knew it, he had his slacks down, trying to get inside of her.

Throughout the struggle, she began to cry, not knowing that turned him on, and as she began to tire, she felt something warm and sticky shoot out all on her thigh. He never stopped pumping until he was satisfied. She was disgusted. He never penetrated, but had nutted all on her leg. Her arms were bruised where he'd held her down, and she cried. She hadn't been there before.

Joy thought Reese would sympathize with her, but he gathered up his important shit and let her know that he thought she was a nasty, fat slut. He let her know he had seen dude in her bed weeks earlier, that she was too wide open for him to be fucking with. He had a wife and couldn't chance catching shit from her. She wasn't what he expected. Truth was, he was tired of her. She was a jump-off that he'd gotten caught up with, and it was time to make an exit.

Joy sat on her bed crying and shaking uncontrollably, as she heard her door slam. She walked out to see her key on the table and embraced the feeling of a lonely apartment.

An hour later, she found herself being treated at Leigh Memorial Hospital for an anxiety attack. Her body raced, her hands shook, and her mouth trembled as tears ran down her face.

Her mother was there trying to find out what brought this on, and her kids were worried to death. Malaina was also there trying to calm her down.

But it wasn't until Lady came in and took both her hands and began to pray, sitting there with her for several hours, did her body start to calm down. The doctor wanted to keep her through the night, but Lady said she would take her home and stay with her.

After Joy got home, and her kids were in bed, and her mother had left, Lady sat talking with her, getting no response. Joy stared at the cable, looking at her stories, praying her body would calm down. She just wanted her hands to stop shaking and the tears to stop forming in her eyes, but that wasn't happening. She was so confused.

Then she heard a knock at the door. For some reason, she got scared, and the anxiety began to build. She waved her hands and head, letting Lady know not to answer the door, that she didn't want to see nobody.

The knocking continued then became a bang.

Lady opened the door to see Omari. He saw Joy on the couch balled up crying, and he walked in slightly, pushing Lady to the side.

"Fuck is wrong with you?" he asked, bewildered.

"She had an anxiety attack. She was over at Leigh Memorial all evening. We just got back," Lady said.

"I'm Omari," he said, holding out his hand to Lady.

"Lady. Nice to meet you." She stared at him, impressed by the young man. She could see why Joy left the party the night he'd called.

"So is my little fat girl gonna be okay?" Omari asked, going over to her and hugging her. He could feel her body trembling. He took both her hands and looked into her eyes. "Hey, I was headed home, and I was deep in thought, smoking this Backwood." He pulled out his Backwood and lit it. "And next thing you know, I'm over here." He laughed.

"It was meant for ya to come by," Lady said.

"I guess my baby needed me."

Omari handed the Backwood to Lady and wrapped his arms around Joy. He held her, she held him back, and her body began to calm down.

After an hour, Lady decided to leave, once Omari said he was staying the night, all Joy needed was to rest, and he was gonna hold her all night, make sure she was okay and got some rest.

Lady kissed Joy, said her good-byes, and was out. "Take care of my girl," were her last words.

Omari took Joy to her room, undressed her, got her in bed, laid down, took her into his arms, and held her close. "I don't know what's worrying you, and exactly all that's going on, but it all ends tonight," he said. "Do you hear me, Joy?"

"Yes," she answered, squeezing him.

"I mean it. I love you. I really do," he said, before falling into a deep sleep.

Over the next several months Joy found peace with Omari. He stayed with her almost every night. He gave her all the attention she needed, but financially she was holding everything down. Omari gave a little, but not enough to give her any security.

After a year of facing hard times, it began to take an effect. Joy began to look at him different. Coming home to a fucked up house, smoking, his Xbox, and hard dick, she felt he'd become like another dependent.

Even when tired, Joy always found the time and energy to give Omari all the love and attention he wanted, but inside, her feelings began to change. Especially when she got into a bind and he couldn't or wouldn't give her a helping hand. Several times her whole check went towards rent and bills, and she had to go to her moms for help.

Along with the help and loan, she had to hear about a nigga laying in her house and her bed, who had nothing to contribute, but she took up for him. Another time when she fell short and didn't have her car payment, she had to go to Malaina, and again along with the loan, she had to hear about a nigga laying up in her shit and not contributing.

Then one time he borrowed her car, ran out all her gas, and then the car broke down. Her being between paydays and being ass out, her son needing money for a school function, and Omari looking at her with his head low, saying he was sorry, but again having nothing to contribute, she had to break down and go to Lady.

CHAPTER 7

It was Lady who broke it down, making her realize that this dude was taking food and money away from her kids, leaving her and the kids fucked up. Her son Juan was getting older and beginning to catch feelings about Omari being there and not playing the role of a father. He brought it to his mom's attention that this dude was holding her back, but her love was so deep and so genuine, she still couldn't let go. But after getting her car fixed a couple times, and putting so much money into it, when the transmission went, she was done.

She sat at home crying, not knowing what to do, so she finally broke down and called Mike, a dude she'd met on Tagged and had a deep infatuation with.

When they met, he came at her on some sincere shit. His mother had passed away with cancer, so he had his page dedicated to cancer awareness, and being a touching subject to Joy and her family, it opened her heart to him, and a door. Mike was supposed to be going through a divorce, so her heart just automatically opened, figuring he had no one to turn to. And when he came at her, requesting friendship, he didn't come as if he wanted anything from her, except an ear to listen to his many problems. He'd gone through hell with his soon-to-be ex-wife, something similar to what she'd gone through with Minke. So they began talking every day and night on the computer.

Joy finally told Mike she wanted to meet him, but he said he didn't want to complicate her life or his at this point. His fifty-first birthday was coming up and he was just learning to deal with all the life changes that had come his way. Even though Mike was older, Joy was really feeling him, because everybody she'd met was only interested in one thing.

She continued talking with him, until one day she heard him mention that he sold cars, and asked him about the dealership. He told her about one of the side-of-the-road dealerships on Military Highway, which she was familiar with.

The following day she worked up the nerve to go up there. She fixed her hair, and threw on a new little pink strapless terrycloth halter top dress. She found her some matching pink sandals from Payless and made her way to his lot at lunchtime. She'd seen Mike's picture online, so when she pulled up, she waited for him to come out and assist her.

As Mike approached her, she stepped out the car. When he smiled, she knew he liked what he saw, but he was tall, big, and flabby, nothing she would normally look at two times. But she knew she'd gotten bigger, older, and wasn't the prize she used to be. Plus, her self-esteem had been crushed by Minke, so any attention was good attention.

Not wanting to appear needy, Joy tried to come across as if she was living well and offered to take him to lunch, thinking it was the beginning of something genuine.

She invited him over later for some good conversation. They'd talked so much online and on the phone, she felt comfortable. When he arrived that evening, they talked, cuddled, smoked, and sipped on the Patrón that Omari had left over there. She felt good that the

old head still puffed like a young'un, and talked like a
young'un, and complimented her, making her feel like
a million.

It had gotten late, so Mike asked if he could relax
with her. It had been a while since he'd held a woman.
He was living with his brother since he had gotten
separated, and was quite lonesome.

Joy wanted the company and she had prepared for
it. Earlier she had washed her sheets, put powder on
them, and sprayed them down with some of the Victo-
ria's Secret body spray. Also, she had douched and cut
the hair down to a sexy triangle on top so that it was
not only sexy to look at but also fresh. When they went
in the room and laid down, she went into the bathroom
and came out wearing a short silk red nightie with a red
robe that she let swing open, allowing him to see her
pride and joy, those forty-two-DDs, and the tattoo on
her thigh that made men weak. Tamil had educated Joy
a lot. She was used to Minke and Minke only since she'd
become a woman. So Tamil made sure she came correct.

When she walked over to the bed, Mike reached out
and hugged her. His hands went straight for her breasts,
which he began to massage and knead as if they were
big rolls of dough. Then he laid her back and took off his
shirt.

Mike was nothing like Minke. He was fat, slouchy,
and had man breasts that Joy knew brought shame
to him, but he stood there as if he had the body of a
dancer.

He leaned over and kissed Joy, sticking his tongue in
her mouth, as if to arouse her, but the wet, sloppy kisses
made her soon turn her head. Joy leaned her head back
so he would kiss her neck. That always moved her.

Soon he had her breasts in his mouth, and was making his way down her body to her stomach. Joy was self-conscious of her belly and size, but after looking at him, she realized she had nothing to be ashamed of.

Mike made his way down to her thigh and began kissing and licking her tattoo. Then he lifted her legs, realizing she wore no panties, and placed his lips on her vagina and began giving her light kisses. He gently licked her clit, and watched it grow and stick out, giving him easy access to take it between his lips and suck on it.

Then he eased his tongue between her swollen lips and into her moist hole, causing her to moan. When he saw her grab the sheets, he lifted her legs higher and put his arms around her thighs, allowing his free hands to push up her stomach, leaving a clear view of all her womanly love. But he went back down to her now wet hole and pushed his tongue so far inside her, she realized she didn't have to douche, he was cleaning her out.

It felt so good, but it didn't compare to him giving her a rim job and licking her ass clean. Joy never knew a man's tongue could get in her asshole, but she found out that night. She wanted to call her momma, but he never stopped. She waited for him to get back to her clit, but he focused on her asshole, wetting it up and putting his fingers inside. It was a bit uncomfortable, but that was his focus.

Mike stood up and dropped his pants. His dick wasn't really hard. He didn't know all this was gonna go down that night, so he wasn't prepared. He had no condoms, and he hadn't taken his blue pill.

He begged her for head, but she denied him, so he eased in her raw, which she allowed, believing he hadn't been nowhere since his wife. He was semi-hard, but after he got in, she felt him begin to swell, and he began to pump. After three minutes she heard him let out a deep moan.

He was done and smiling, beads of sweat sprinkled on his forehead, but he could tell she hadn't cum. He did something that surprised her, that no man had ever done to her: He began eating her again, trying to make her cum after he'd cum in her.

Joy quickly faked an orgasm. She was done. As long as he was happy, she was okay. She just wanted someone to want her, someone to compliment her, someone to keep her company, so she wouldn't have to be alone. And Mike was it. And they laid together and fell asleep.

The next several days Mike showed nothing but concern, as if she had him open. He came to her job and took her to lunch. He came by each evening to keep her company.

Then the weekend came, and he got a room down the beach, where they walked and talked, and took pictures as if they were a couple. They went to the room, sat in the Jacuzzi, and smoked and sipped on Patrón.

Mike began a repeat of the other night, but tonight he paid all the attention to her asshole, licking and sucking it raw. He pulled some liquid KY from his bag and put on his finger, to ease in and out of her ass. Joy didn't care too much for it, but it made him happy. Then he grabbed a condom. Tonight he was ready. His dick stood straight up.

He eased inside of her then turned her over as he hit from the back. Then he slid his finger in her ass before pulling out, putting some KY on his dick, and trying to ease in her ass. She jumped, but he held her, letting her know that it might hurt a little but he was a pro at it. Fucking in the ass was his thing.

Joy was hurting, but she wanted so much to satisfy him, she did what he wanted. And Mike never saw the tears in her eyes from the pain, but she didn't want him to leave her. Over the next few months, they got closer, and Joy noticed he just loved to eat her then go straight to her asshole. In fact, he'd cum in her ass much more than in her vagina.

One day, while Mike was chilling at her house, she was preparing to get a shower, trying to get ready for one of their escapades. She forgot her shower cap, so she yelled for him in the living room, but her call went unanswered. She wrapped a towel around her and walked out the bathroom, but didn't see him. She went to the door and opened it, hearing him on the phone outside her apartment door. She quickly shut the door and went to the window and cracked it.

"Naw, baby, can I get this money? I gotta work late, so I can finish this paperwork, so I can make this extra change. If I don't, who gonna pay the mortgage? We already behind," he said. "Soon as I finish this paper-work, I got another customer. And you know I can't afford to let nothing slip by me. Love ya now. I'll be home in a bit. Put me a plate in the microwave. Love ya. Later!"

Joy ran back in the room and into the bathroom.

Mike came back inside. "You all right, baby?" he yelled.

"Yeah!" she said through the pain.

Then she heard the front door open and shut again. She walked back to the window.

"What up, bro? What you doing?" Mike asked on the phone.

"Who? Tamil? She over there now? Sucking dick? Nasty bitch!" he said, laughing. "When we gonna fuck her again? She think because she turned me on to this fat bitch, I don't want no more of that white pussy, but her roommate don't suck dick on a reg."

Mike listened for a bit then said, "Nigga, shit! You know me. Don't make me a difference, man or woman, boy or girl. I'll fuck 'em all in the ass. Keeps my KY jelly to lube 'em up." He laughed hard. "At the end of the day, you know I carry my ass home to my wife. Fuck these hoes and these gay-ass niggas! Nobody ain't getting in *my* ass," he said seriously. "I'll be there in a few. This bitch in the shower. Soon as she come out, I'ma get this quick nut and I'm out. Tell Tam thanks for the hookup. Holla in a bit, man."

Joy ran to the shower and allowed the water to camouflage her tears. She didn't know what to do, but it quickly hit her.

When they'd first met online and started talking, they had gotten close, and one week he called and she really couldn't talk because she was in so much pain from her period coming down. So Tamil had told him she would have to call him back. When they did talk, he acted so concerned about her monthly pain. She even remembered him making a comment about the shit women have to go through, but actually she was one of those women who only got a period twice a year, and then she had to make it come on. She hadn't had one since they'd been fucking around and remembered he went raw the first time, and a couple times after that in her pussy and in her ass.

She got out the shower and dried off, grabbed her purple robe and slipped it on. Soon as she walked out, he grabbed her from behind.

"What up, baby? You know I miss ya. Been on my mind all day. Couldn't wait to get to ya," he said, pants off, dick in his hand already lubed up with the KY, and his right hand looking greasy.

He quickly slid his hand under her robe, and before she knew it, she was on her bed, face down, his hand in the crack of her ass, and his middle finger easing in her asshole. She turned quickly and sat down, holding her stomach, looking at him, his manhood sticking straight up and his hand in an upward position.

"What's wrong?" he asked, not used to her stopping him.

"My stomach been fucked up. I know this feeling. I think I'm pregnant, Mike."

"Pregnant? What?"

Joy watched his dick go soft.

"Yeah, baby. It's a blessing. Your mother passed away about a year ago. This could be her way of sending you someone to really love and call your own. I'm getting over my ex, you're getting over your past. This is gonna be our connection," she said, staring in his face. "I love you." Joy smiled. "Come make love to me," she said, pulling off her robe, laying back, and spreading her legs. "Let me feel you in here." She brushed her hand across her vagina and stomach, not caring about him seeing her belly.

"You sure, Joy? 'Cause I ain't ready for no baby. You got kids and me too. This ain't the time."

"Mike, don't do this. Please don't do this. I love you, Mike. I wanna keep it. I want us to be together, to be a family." Joy began to cry.

"Baby, I got to figure this out. Damn! I didn't mean for this to happen," he said, putting his underwear and slacks back on.

"Please don't make me go through this by myself. We a family."

"I got to think, baby. I got to put this together. Give me a few. I got to get up to the lot." He kissed her and gave her a hug.

She placed his hand on her stomach. "We love you. Will I see you later?"

"Yeah!" he answered and was out the door.

Joy saw him once more after that, a week later, when he dropped off $700 for her to get an abortion and then get a room for a couple days so they could have some privacy to deal with the situation. They hadn't talked since.

Now she was calling him to help her get a car. But her license and credit weren't good, so she was gonna have to get it in Omari's name. To her surprise, Omari gave her $1,500 down. Mike took it to a couple finance companies he worked hand in hand with and got it done, and they drove off with a new Impala.

The $1,500 rekindled what she felt for Omari, and for another year, she put up with him and the shit that came with it. But when her lease was up and she wanted to move, Omari was doing bad, and she needed some help.

Joy eventually found a place, a three-bedroom town house, in a section of VA Beach called Lake Edward. She could handle the $800 monthly rent, but she didn't have $1,600 to get in the place. She had two weeks to move out of her place, and her back was against the wall. She did everything she could to get the money, but nothing, and nobody, came through.

She tried to force Omari, giving him an ultimatum, making her home as uncomfortable as possible. She stopped cooking, packed up all the dishes, stopped fucking him, and even had other niggas calling the house.

Omari was furious. He had nothing to give, so he began staying back at his moms more, but never gave up on Joy.

Joy stayed on her grind, but she couldn't find this money nowhere. She swore she would never be without again. Not wanting to go to her moms, she went to her last resort, Brooklyn Cuts.

CHAPTER 8

Minke had turned most of his drug money into legitimate businesses, opening up a barber shop, rim shop, and a restaurant. But he couldn't stay out the streets. They had him. They were who he was married to.

Joy had gotten right this day, making sure that when Minke saw her, he would definitely want some pussy. As she got closer to the shop, her stomach kept churning. She hadn't seen him since he shitted on her, and she hadn't talked to him, but through the grapevine, she'd heard what he was up to. She even knew in the last six years, he'd been locked up for two, but came home and got his shit back. He had caught his charge in VA and was sent up to Indian Creek. She thought he was gonna try to reach out to her then and she could get the chance to shit on him and pay him back, but he never did.

She walked inside Brooklyn Cuts, wearing a white flowing skirt, navy blue open-toe sandals with three-inch heels, and a navy blue shirt with the top buttons open, showing her forty-two-DD's being held by the navy blue bra. Lady had weaved her head up so that the wrap was super tight as it came around and rested on her chest.

Every barber's mouth dropped at the big girl coming in, even Sizemo, who was cutting in the first chair. When he realized it was Joy, he stopped staring, and they hugged each other.

Sizemo was Minke's man, running all his shit while he was away and out of town. He was with Minke and Hitler the day they'd met her, Malaina, and Queen.

He stared at her up and down again, and then at her breasts. They looked as if they were trying to get at him. "Gotdamn, girl! Got me ready to snatch you up," he joked.

He knew she would always be Minke's girl, but if she let him, he would fuck her. She was always like that to him since the first day he saw her, and now that extra weight meant nothing. After twelve years, who hadn't gotten bigger? He was a 200 solid beast when she last saw him, now he was pushing 350, mostly fat.

"Where my baby daddy at, boy? You crazy."

"In New York," he said.

"Well, I need you to get him a message for me. Can you do that?"

"Yeah. Fuck you been up to? Don't act like we strangers, girl. We done hung. You used to stop by and holla, even when you and Minke was together. He ain't never mind you coming by, smoking and hanging with the god. Don't get new!" Sizemo smirked.

"I know. You know we always been cool, Sizemo. You know I been through it."

"All right, all right. What you doing later?" he asked, not wanting her to get started on personal shit in the shop. "Well, hold tight. I'll be finished in a few. We can put one in the air and catch up."

"Sounds good. Hope you gonna feed me," she said seriously. "Shit! Ain't nothing change."

"Give me a second," he said smiling and shaking his head.

When Sizemo finished his last appointment, him and Joy jumped in his Tahoe and headed to Applebee's. As soon as they got in the truck, the sounds began to blast, and he lit the Dutch that sat in the ashtray.

"Ain't nothing change, baby, but the weight." Sizemo passed her the slow-burning Dutch.

"I see, nigga. You know I know how you do." She laughed. "I also know you better not make me fuck a bitch up for rolling in the street with ya. Know you still running hoes." She laughed as she passed the Dutch back.

"Naw, ain't shit change, but now I want my own bitch. Got to have my own," he said.

"So whatever happened to Pat? That was yo' bitch. You two muthafuckas used to go at it."

"You ain't lying. She was one of the good ones, but you know, I felt I made a better choice when I met Rhonda. And I did. Then I felt I did better when I met Carmen. And I did. Then came Lelani, and she was the fucking bomb. But ain't none of them hoes make me marry 'em. So then came Kamrin. Kam-Kam. That's my baby. She at work right now. RN. Bitch really got it going on, so I'm moving slow right now," he said seriously.

"Shit, yo big ass ain't got no choice but to move slow."

"Look who talking. When you walked in the shop, I was like, *Damn! Who's this wobbling in here with those big-ass titties?*" Sizemo laughed as he parked.

"Shit! Nigga, I was like, *Who this fat dike-bitch with big-ass titties?* Then I said, *Oh God, that's Sizemo.* Nigga, you need a bra." Joy laughed.

"Fuck you, girl! But yo' ass right. I should've been back in the gym. This shit is pathetic," he said, grabbing his stomach and chest. "And now both our big asses going in here and get bigger."

Sizemo and Joy bust out laughing together.

She closed the door. "Niggas still on the cute face and begging to touch the girls."

"And bitches still giving me pussy and fighting over this dick, so I'm all right."

"Picture yo big ass fucking. All them hoes see is money. The cool fat guy in the Jordans, Rocawear gear, New York fitted, pushing the nice truck, and they see money." Joy smirked.

"All they better see is this dick, because that's all a nigga giving away," he said, smiling as they sat down.

"You right. You ain't change."

"Never will, my nigga, never will. Let's sit at the bar. Double Patrón!" he yelled as he sat down. "What you want, Joy?"

"Same thing, nigga. If I'm hanging, I'm chilling."

"That's what it is. Know what? When we leave here, I got to go to MacArthur Mall. I got to get my shorty a birthday gift. You with me?"

"Hell, yeah! I ain't got shit to do today." Joy was feeling good about hanging out and having a nice time with a real friend.

"So what's the deal with you? What you been up to, Joy? Where you been? And what made you come up in yo' husband shop?"

"That nigga ain't my husband. He's my kids' father. My baby daddy," she said with a smirk. "But I need him now. I ain't came at him in years, but my back against the wall," she said, staring out in space.

"Well, what's the word you want me to get to him?"

"I ain't one of his bitches, trying to hunt this nigga down because he won't return my call. I was his wife, I had his kids. This muthafucka decided to just shit on me and his kids one day and left me fucked up. I made it through, and made sure these kids kept food in they mouth and a roof over their head, but I need some help. My lease up, and I need some dough to make this next move."

Sizemo smiled. "And you say all that to say?"

"Call that nigga up. You got that direct line Size. Don't play. Hit him now," Joy said seriously.

Sizemo pulled out his phone and dialed Minke, who answered on the second ring.

"What it do, my dude?"

"You know . . . what I hit you about, it's good?" Sizemo asked.

"Yeah, yeah, perfect timing. Put her on," Minke said, his stomach feeling funny.

"Here ya go." Sizemo handed Joy the phone.

"Hello." Joy's stomach was churning too. She didn't know why she was feeling funny about talking to him, and her voice had a slight crack in it.

"What's up, mommy? How you doing today?"

"I'm doing good today. And you, Minke?"

"Okay now," he said softly. "I went through it for a sec, but getting back on my feet."

"You back, nigga, and running."

"You crazy, Lecia," he said in a soft Northern tone.

Nobody called her Lecia but him. Her whole world became a daze, as she listened.

"What I'm trying to figure out, what the fuck going on in your life that would make you come look for me?"

"Well, I got a two-bedroom off Little Creek. Your son is too big to be sharing a room with his sister," she said, stepping away from the bar and going outside. "Excuse me, I had to walk outside. Don't need everybody in my business."

"You got business now?" he asked, laughing.

"You made me get some business. Or fucking drown!"

"Why you cussin', Lecia? See, you getting fucking mad. Then that attitude shit come out, and—"

"And what? What, Minke? You left me fucked up, and I ain't supposed to have no attitude? Tell me this, muthafucka!"

And for twenty minutes straight, it seemed, without taking a breath, she went through all his wrong, her shelter life, her moms' house, and her struggles with two kids. She was breathing hard, ready to cry.

"And all that ended in divorce. You said it, I heard it, and maybe I deserve that. But that's the last time I want to hear it. And let that be the last time you ever disrespect me by calling me out my name."

"Fuck you, Minke! You ain't shit," Joy said, forgetting everything. "You can't do shit else to hurt me. You can't—"

"Hey!" he yelled. "You got me fucked up, bitch! I will come down there and beat yo muthafuckin' ass! Wife or not, try me, Lecia! Test me!" he said loudly.

They shared a moment of silence.

"You ain't gonna put yo hands on me," she said softly.

He mocked her. "*You ain't gonna put yo hands on me.* Shut your country ass up! What's up? What you need?" he asked directly.

"I need to move by the first, and I need two thousand dollars."

"Where you moving to?"

"Lake Edward. Town house, three-bedroom on East Hastings. It's eight fifty a month, but I got to pay water, get shit on, you know."

"When you gonna give me my money back?" he asked, holding in his laugh.

"Minke, please. You owe—" was all she got out.

"Fuckin' wit' cha! Check this. I'll pay the security deposit and three months rent . . . if you got me. I need a spot to crash for a second."

"Yeah, Minke," she said, knowing he ain't need her place, but just wanted to control some shit. *Niggas pay like they weight*, she thought. *That's how they roll in his world.*

"Call me on your phone." And he gave her his number.

She did it, and now they were on her phone.

"Lock me in. I'm gonna hit you later and let you know when I'll be in town."

"Okay," she said softly.

"Love ya, Lecia," he said softly.

Joy smiled. "Yeah, right." She walked back inside to see Sizemo eating, and her food sitting there. "Here's your phone. Thank you," she said, smiling.

"You better not had got the number off my phone."

"He gave it to me."

"Oh! Shit, don't y'all call me when he come in town and y'all wilding out. I had enough of that shit."

"Nobody argued more than Queen and Hitler. That's who you had to keep from killing each other." Joy laughed.

"Literally from killing each other, and in the end, they killed each other." Sizemo laughed, but Joy didn't.

They finished eating, and they talked all the way to the mall, where Joy helped Sizemo pick out a Coach bag and shoes for Kamrin, his new love.

The day went fast.

Sizemo took her back to get her car and told her to come by and hit another Dutch. She did, and also got a chance to meet Kamrin. It was a day she enjoyed. She hadn't had a day like that in a while.

Joy went home envying the way Sizemo talked about his love for the woman in his life. Minke was the only man to ever love her like that. She hadn't seen love like that since him. It actually made her anxious. She couldn't wait to see him. She fell asleep trying to think of every reason she should hate him, but she couldn't. And she didn't know why. She fell asleep that night with Minke on her mind, and tears in her heart.

The next morning Joy woke to the ringing of her phone. It was Omari. She knew it was an argument on the other end, so she ignored him. She got up and jumped in the shower then came out to get dressed. She saw she'd missed several calls. When it rang again, she picked up.

"Hello," she said. "I'm trying to get dressed, boy. What's up?"

"Fuck you mean, what's up?" he yelled. "Don't gaff me off! I saw you with that nigga yesterday! You driving niggas around in my shit!"

"Fuck you, Omari! It ain't yo business what the fuck I do. And, nigga, you ain't made not one payment on shit. Get the fuck outta here!"

"Well, I made it my business, and you won't be riding and fucking the next nigga in my shit, bitch!" he said and hung up.

Joy called him back, but he didn't answer. After several attempts, he picked up.

"What?"

"Kill that shit, Omari. That's my shit. I made the payments and fixed it when it broke. I pay the insurance, taxes. Come on, son, I even let you drive it. That's my shit, so kill that." Joy couldn't believe he was coming at her like that.

"Come on, son," he said laughing. "You back on that New York shit. You on that slick shit now. Y'all bitches think ya slick—'til ya ass in a sling! But don't underestimate this Norfolk nigga, baby. I gave my all and you shitted on me. Now you gonna see how I really get down. Stanking-ass, nasty, fat bitch!"

Joy listened in complete silence to the cruel comments.

"I can't believe you did this shit to me," she heard him say in a whining voice.

"Nigga, you must have lost your mind. You got me fucked up. I'm tired of this going-without shit, and nigga, you are not a contributor. You ain't even a damn sponsor. A sponsor can give anything. You don't give me shit, and it's come-up time. Done with ya, son!" she yelled and hung up.

Joy felt like a weight had been lifted off her. She felt free.

She finished getting herself together and looked in the mirror. "God, I thank You for all You do, all You've done, and all You gonna do. Look over my family, and God, please put Your arms around me and keep me safe. Amen." She smiled.

She grabbed her purse and keys and headed out, but when she reached the parking lot, her smile disappeared. Like being hit with a sledgehammer. Her car was gone. She ran in the house mad as hell with tears in her eyes. She picked up her phone and called Omari, but he never answered. After the twentieth time, she gave up.

"What up, Ma?" she heard her son say. Her still being home was unusual. He could tell something was wrong.

"Nothing, Juan. Just trying to find a ride to work."

"Omari got the whip? That fool know you got to go to work. Call Dad," he said, leaving out the door. As he opened the door, he waited for the normal response, "When hell freeze over. Yo' daddy's dead," but it never came. Him and his sister knew their dad wasn't dead, because when she got fucked up, she would tell them good things about him. And when she heard he was locked up, she'd allowed Sizemo to carry them to see him one time.

"I don't know, Juan. I might. I'm tired," she said, not wanting to tell him she'd talked to him, just in case he didn't show.

"Sound good, Ma. He said he was coming home to a different life when he was locked up."

"That's prison talk. Your dad is a hustler. It's in him through and through," she said seriously.

"See ya later, Ma," he said, closing the door.

"Love ya, baby." Joy picked up her phone. "Hello?"

"What up, girl? Better hype your ass up this morning." Sizemo laughed. He didn't get the response he thought he would.

"I'm okay," she said sadly.

"No, you not. What's up?" he asked sternly.

"Lost my car, Sizemo. Muthafucka took my car."

"My people thought you were getting shit straight. Actually, I thought you had it straight."

"Why would you think that?" she asked, wondering how he could have come up with that.

"When you talk to a boss for a half an hour on the phone, all your problems should be over. Ain't that right, baby?" he asked, directing his question to his girl Kamrin, but talking to Joy.

"Yeah, right!" Kam said, not paying him much attention.

"Oh, you ain't straight, girl?" he yelled at Kam.

"Yeah, I'm straight, nigga, because I carry my ass to work every day. I don't know who you trying to front on. If you boss, nigga, let me take the rest of the week off. You got me? Huh? You got me?" she repeated. "Thought so. You took too long."

"Shut the hell up! You know what it is," Sizemo said.

"No, I don't, but you can tell me later. I don't want to hear that shit now," Kamrin said.

"So how you getting to work?" he asked Joy.

"Shit, I'm gonna have to take a day. Not good, but . . ."

"Me and my girl on the way to the gym, but I got you," he said. "Where you at?"

Joy gave him directions. She was outside when he arrived.

"Thanks, son," she said, climbing in the back.

"Joy, you remember Kamrin?"

"Nice to meet you again. How are you?"

"Not good. I'm trying to calm down. My shit was fucked up, so I got my car in my dude name. He put up the fifteen hundred, but I been paying for it, and keeping it up. He got mad and took my shit while I was 'sleep.'"

"He ain't mad, girl, he hurt," Kamrin said.

"Like I told you yesterday, get your shit right and make sure you can always hold your own shit down. Joy, we go back how many years?"

"About fourteen years, son. When you were out here destroying niggas, when you were a beast, when all this was solid," she said, reaching up front, hitting his chest.

"My teddy bear wa'n't no beast. He's soft." Kamrin rubbed his stomach.

"She don't know about that life, Joy," Sizemo said. "My point was, as a friend, I'm telling you, get your shit right, and don't depend on a muthafuckin' soul. Not your man, not your family. Depend on yourself, do for self, and you won't never find yourself fucked up. A true friend that come one hundred all the time is hard, real hard, to find."

"You don't have to tell me. I've been through it, and this is a lesson well learned. My mom tried to tell me, but I didn't listen, but I came to learn," she said as they reached her job.

"You good?" Sizemo asked.

"Thanks, son. Really appreciate it," Joy said. "And it was nice meeting you again," she said to Kamrin.

"Same here. Hope to see you again." Kamrin was feeling funny that Sizemo would cut her off from talking about who he used to be. She actually hated the fact that he had a friend who knew more about her man than she did.

"So what's on your mind?" Sizemo asked as they headed to the gym. "You ain't saying shit."

"Nothing. I'm good."

"Keep it one hundred, baby. That's how our shit stay good."

"I don't like other bitches knowing more about my dude than me. You say she's Minke girl. You talk about her like she your ex, and she know you, really know you. I need to know you, not just what you show me," she said, looking straight at him.

"You know me and Minke history. She been around since the beginning. I've always been the nigga to hold shit down in his or Hitler absence. I took care of everything and even his family. We been tight for a long time. Me and Joy spent a lot of time smoking, hanging out, and taking care of certain shit. We had to put trust in each other, and when Hitler got killed and Minke pulled me in closer, all three of us got closer. Then something happened between him and Joy. He started running around and doing shit I had never seen him do—fucking with bitches, staying out of town a lot—and she leaned on me. Many days she sat in my house, chilling, smoking, and she would be hurting, crying, but trying to get through it. She leaned on me a lot, but I always respected my man and kept mad respect for her."

"So you never fucked her? Things happen late at night, especially when a girl is hurting and vulnerable," Kamrin said, knowing she'd been through similar shit.

"Naw, it never went there. I was just there for her," he said nonchalantly.

"I don't know, Sizemo. I would think something might have happened. I know Minke. Can you tell me he never thought shit might be going on? He never questioned that shit?" Kamrin smiled.

"Yeah, he did. And one day I told him, 'Man, I'm mad close to her too, and I wa'n't gonna turn my back on her for nothing because wa'n't nothing going on. But when they broke up for real and he exed her out of his life for good, he told me why, and he told me that if I wanted to keep getting this money with him, he had to know that me and him was one hundred, and he didn't want to feel or think a certain way over his wife. So he said I had to make a choice," Sizemo said, looking at her. "And I tell you the same thing I told him then, 'She is a friend, and I don't look at her like that,'" he quoted seriously. "We stopped talking for years, but we still cool. Actually, it was good to see her."

"Okay, I got to take your word. Like you say, nigga always keep it one hundred. You got no reason to lie to me. You have no reason," she said.

Sizemo walked in the gym, knowing Joy was going to trip off this shit later.

Joy's day turned out quite well. Omari still hadn't answered the phone, but there was a lady she had befriended at work, and she was gonna find out just how much of a friend she'd become. Joy had told her about her situation, and she had offered to take her home and pick her up the following morning, but Joy had to roll to Luxury Brown for the afterwork party. Joy agreed, and to her surprise, they had male dancers performing, something she wasn't really into. She called Malaina and Lady, not knowing if they were going to show up.

She was having a nice time with Kim and some of the other girls from work, but when her girls walked in, her spirits escalated to the next level. And the party began as soon as Malaina ordered a round for them as she approached the table.

"Let's get it in, girl. Order up," she told Joy, Kim, and Lady.

"Malaina, this is Kim and Lady," Joy introduced.

"What up? Tell the waitress what y'all want. I got first round," Malaina said cheerfully.

"Patrón," Joy said.

"Eighteen hundred," Malaina said.

"Hennessy," Kim said.

"Make that two Hennessys," Lady said, and the foursome was set off.

By the third round and the last dancer, the girls were up, hyped, and talking mad shit.

"How much was that last round, girl?" Lady asked Kim.

"Thirty-six."

Lady peeled off two twenties and a five to slide on the tray as the waitress walked up. "Here we go," Lady said as everyone grabbed their drink.

"Why those niggas keep coming over here dancing in front of Kim?" Joy yelled. "Is it because she sliding them niggas fives?" She laughed and gave Malaina a high-five.

"Shit! Them niggas like those big-ass titties. Thought my shits were big," Malaina said.

They all laughed.

"Big titties and that beautiful-ass face. Girl, you are what niggas call gorgeous," Lady said smiling as they watched the next dancer come to the stage.

"Niggas can eat some of this gorgeous pussy. Wrap these fat-ass thighs around his muthafuckin' neck." Kim high-fived Lady.

"Now inhale that clit and breathe," Lady added, laughing.

They all fell out, the liquor taking control.

"Bitch-ass nigga!" Joy said, keeping the laughter going.

Lady looked over at Kim in her khaki-colored fitted Chanel skirt, cream open-toe Chanel sandals with four-inch heels, and the cream, silk see-through blouse that showed her cream-colored bra that set her forty-DD's up and out. Lady smiled, her eyes going from her breasts to her light, flawless skin, small lips, high cheekbones, slanted eyes, and the long, silky black hair that came from her mixed background. Lady took in the whole package as Gee XXL danced in front of her. She had a belly and no ass, but her total package demanded attention because she came across as a big, beautiful, classy diva.

As Gee XXL made his way to the next table, Lady said loud enough for her girls to hear, "Carry your gay ass."

"Is he gay, girl?" Malaina asked.

"That first nigga was his man. Seen them niggas together at a couple parties, one of the gay niggas in the shop has. That probably ain't all his dick," she added.

"The hell, it ain't. I gave him some pussy after he ate this one night about two months ago. Nigga got about ten inches of dick that wouldn't stay hard. He told me it was because he don't like condoms. I ain't give a fuck. I pushed the Magnum on and pushed that semi-hard dick in my pussy. I was wet as hell. Had a good time. But he ain't never call back, and I didn't care. On to the next one." Kim slapped high-five with Malaina, who was all in her mouth.

Joy looked at her like she was surprised.

"Shit, I work hard and I play hard. Who stroke that gee a month for that fly-ass condo? Me! Who stroke that check for that new AC? Me! Fuck these niggas! They can eat my pussy and suck my ass then carry they ass. I'm done!" she said, dancing around.

"Heard that shit. I ain't got my own shit, but y'all and this shit here just became part of my getaway. My friend supposed to be coming up here later," Malaina said.

"Who?" Joy asked, looking at her.

"Fat Boy, Reese partner," Malaina said as they looked on.

"You still talk to him?" Joy asked, surprised.

"Please. That's my dude. That nigga funny. He always got trees, and we fuck anywhere. In the car, his cousin crib, momma house, daddy house, backyard, garage, closet. That nigga off the chain." Malaina was shaking her head, smiling.

"Bitch, I gots to be comfortable," Lady said. "Get a room, nigga."

The other girls agreed.

"Shit, I ain't got all that time. Give me mine, so I can go home to my husband and carry my ass to sleep," she said laughing.

They all finished their drinks and looked at Joy.

She told them, "I ain't got shit in this purse, but condoms for a good piece," and they all broke out laughing.

"Bring another round," Malaina told their waitress. "Shit! I ain't had no real fun in a minute."

"For real. Whoa!" Kim yelled as the slow music came flowing through the speakers and the lights went low.

The women who had been there before knew it was the last dance of the night and they always saved the best for last. As the smoke cleared across the dance floor, the voice over the music announced Big Booby.

The waitress sitting the drinks on the table broke their concentration long enough for Lady to throw a twenty on the table, followed by Malaina's twenty. Then Kim tossed one of the tens she had in her hand for Big Booby, got her drink, and everyone's focus went back to Booby.

Booby stood in place, with his head down and the blue fitted pulled low. He wore no shirt, allowing his 220 pounds of pure muscle to be admired by the women in the club. His smooth, dark skin was making the women melt. He lifted his head and took off his hat and threw it on the table where Joy and them sat, allowing the women to look at his shiny baldy and the perfectly trimmed goatee that surrounded the bright smile he flashed only for a second, and the ladies began to scream.

Booby stomped his way forward to one of the tables and began to move his body in a seductive motion, letting his jeans slide off his hips a little more. Then he grabbed them and stomped the Timbs across to the other side for another set of ladies. He gyrated his hips and threw his leg on the table, putting his pelvic region in the lady's face and pumping. The woman's screams escalated, and the money rained. He held his left leg out, his Timbs in the air, and the lady snatched off his boot. Then he stepped back, and the right leg went straight out. He held his balance, showing his coordination skills, as the other lady snatched off his other boot.

Booby slid in front of the table where the girls sat and stared into Joy's eyes as he danced. He fell back on his ass, placed his hands on the floor, and lifted himself off the floor, holding his legs straight out with only his hands on the floor, every muscle in his arms and shoulders bulging.

Kim grabbed the bottom of his pants and snatched them off, leaving him with only his black bikini drawers.

He flipped over and humped the hard floor as if he was making love, and when he jumped to his feet, the women came with screams and chaos. They all stared at the big-ass bulge of soft dick trying to set itself free from the tight bikinis.

Booby eased over to Joy and danced. He could see the discomfort in her face. He leaned down, putting his head on her chest, acting as if he was licking her neck, but came up to her ear.

"Relax, baby. Before you leave, I need to tell you something. Don't leave before we get a chance to talk." He smiled at her as he backed up.

Then he got on his knees and crawled up to Kim. He licked her leg from her ankle to her thigh. Kim opened her legs, revealing her cream thong, and he pushed his face in her crotch. The club erupted. Even Kim and the girls screamed.

Booby got up, getting his jeans and Timbs, and broke out to the back amid the chaos.

The DJ changed the music, and a lot of the women began to leave, except for those who wanted to club, because they began to let the guys come in and the party had begun.

"I'm outta here, ladies. I got an early start and a long-ass day tomorrow. Nice meeting you, Kim," Lady said, giving her a hug. "And you too, Malaina." Lady extended her arms toward Malaina, and they hugged.

"Be right back." Joy walked with Lady outside to her car. "You all right to get home?" she asked.

"No doubt. You be easy, and call me tomorrow," Lady said with another hug. "Love ya."

"Love you too, Lady." Joy smiled and made her way back in the club. When she came back in, Fat Boy, Reese, and Ray was standing around Malaina and Kim, talking.

"What up, niggas?" Joy asked as she approached.

"It's all good," Fat Boy said.

"You know what it is," Reese added.

Joy just stared at him. She knew he felt something for her because she felt funny in his presence.

"Sorry for the things I said. I was hurt. Even though I got my situation, I was still hurt. Just want you to know. Hope we can still be cool," Reese said.

"Boy, we all right. We had our time, and I enjoyed it. We cool," she said with a smile. "Your girl got a good nigga," she added, touching his arm. "Try to stay on the right path."

Joy saw Booby coming out the back and eased to the other side of Kim, making sure he knew them niggas were with Malaina, not her and Kim.

Booby walked over to Kim and Joy. "What up, ladies? Enjoyed the show?" he asked with his million-dollar smile.

"As always, Big Booby!" Kim said, giving him a half-hug.

"You did your thing," Joy said, smiling at him.

He smiled back. "I like you. What's your name?"

"Alecia, and this Kim," Joy answered.

"Well, I've met Kim. She hold me down. She good peeps," he said, smiling at Kim. "Just so that you know, Alecia, I never mess with these women I dance for, but I like you, and I want some of your time. Can I get your number?"

Joy had a question mark on her face. She didn't feel like he was shit to mess with. She figured he was fucking mad girls, especially out here dancing.

"Check it. Here's my card." Then he took out a pen and wrote his number on the back. "Call me at home, so we can talk," he said, handing her his card.

"No doubt. That's a promise." Joy was feeling better that he'd left it up to her.

Booby leaned over and whispered something in Kim's ear, while looking at Joy, so she would know he was talking about her. Then he made his exit.

"Ready, or you want to stay awhile?" Kim asked.

"I'm ready," Joy answered. "What you gonna do, Malaina?"

"I'm good. I'm out. Going over here with Fat Boy for about an hour. Then you know what it is." Malaina smiled.

"I can drop you off, roll up one, and chill out a minute, Joy." Looking at Joy made Reese want to go up to her and wrap his arms around her and squeeze. He missed her. He had that sexiness at the crib that he loved with all his heart, but being with Joy was something he couldn't comprehend. She was soft, cuddly, plump, with full breasts to play with, and the pussy got soaking wet. It was nothing like being with her.

"Naw, I'm good. Call me later, Malaina, when you on your way home. See y'all later," Joy said as her and Kim left.

No sooner than Joy was in the house, all her problems sat back on her shoulders. She began to blow Omari's phone up, but he didn't answer. She knew all he wanted was to come back over there with her, but that wouldn't happen unless Minke didn't come through and she had to stay living in her crutched-up two-bedroom apartment. She needed her car. If she just gave in and let him fuck, she would have it back, but she was tired of begging, tired of these nothing-ass niggas she called friends, who only wanted to look out for themselves. She'd rather be by herself than deal with the bullshit. She was coming to the realization that niggas were gonna be around, holding their dick, ready to fuck, no matter what. But what else did they come with? What else did they have to offer?

Kim pulled up at her condo to see the black Nissan Titan sitting on twenty-two's parked in guest parking. By the time she made it to her door and turned the key, she felt the muscular arms wrap around her body.

Booby locked her door as she turned towards him, and he kissed her. As she allowed his tongue to explore the inside of her mouth, he unbuttoned her cream shirt and threw it to the side. He reached down and pulled the tight khaki skirt up to her waist. He slowed down, putting fingers on both sides of her thong, and pulled it off.

Kim leaned back on the arm of the chair as Booby fell to his knees and buried his face in her crotch and began lapping like a dog that hadn't had nothing to drink all day.

"Can I just freshen up? I ain't showered since this morning, and I've been going all day, Booby. Aaah-hhh!" She felt his tongue go insde of her, making her lift her sizeable legs up off the floor and spread them for him.

"No, I'm being nasty tonight. I'll lick you clean." He buried his face back into her hot, moist, musty pussy. His eyes caught a view of her sandals that she still had on, and that gave him some extra stiffness.

Every time Booby tried to lick or suck her clit, Kim took both her hands and pushed his head down to where he was just licking her womanhood. She didn't want him on her clit. She wasn't trying to cum just yet.

But after fifteen minutes, she was yelling, "Eat that pussy, Booby, eat that pussy," spreading her legs as far open as she possibly could. "I'm horny as shit, Booby. Make me cum."

"Baby, do you feel it? Get ready and cum for me. Tonight I want you to do whatever you want, Kim. Do what you want, *Mami*," he said, hoping.

Kim smiled. She knew where the night was going.

Booby undid her bra, releasing her hefty bust. Then he reached up and took her large, hardened nipples between his fingers and squeezed them lightly. He heard and felt her breathing increase, and her thighs began to close on his head. He'd been there before and was ready for the squeeze from her large thighs.

He pushed his tongue deep into her and flipped it all around, holding his breath, applying more pressure to her nipples.

Kim yelled as if she didn't care who heard her cumming. She fell back and relaxed.

Booby got up and removed his clothes, and headed for the shower.

Kim removed her skirt and shoes, and reached in her drawer where she kept her toys and videos. She threw in the video she knew he liked and lit a Newport.

"Look in my pocket and set it up," Booby yelled from the bathroom as he dried off.

Kim took the valve out and dumped the cocaine on the dresser, cutting it into four lines. She snorted two, and he came out and immediately did his two, hugged her, and they fell on the bed.

She took over, kissing him slowly. She could taste and smell her own pussy, which actually turned her on. Then she kissed his neck, allowing her tongue and lips to lick and suck simultaneously.

Booby's body tightened as she continued her way down to his chest and nipples. As she licked and sucked on his nipples, she listened to this breathing get more intense. She grabbed his dick and began to massage and stroke it then lightly rub the tip. Booby's dick got so hard, it began to jump.

Kim smiled, knowing he was ready. She eased down his stomach and instantly took the head of his manhood into her mouth and licked in a circular motion. Then she took it into her mouth and began her sucking motion, allowing a lot of saliva to run down his shaft, onto his balls, and into his ass-crack.

Kim moved faster, sucking and licking his entire shaft, from the tip of his dick down to his asshole. She rubbed his ass as he lifted his legs up, spread his ass cheeks with both hands, and stuck her tongue in his ass, causing him to jump.

Her tongue went to work, in and out, across it, sucked on it, as he panted, then went back to his balls, then took the head back into her mouth.

Every time she allowed her middle finger to go across his asshole, he jumped. She felt him tighten up, until her finger slid into his ass, and he accepted it. She sucked while she pressed her finger against his prostate, and he shook his head and gasped for breath, ecstasy taking over his body.

Kim reached over to her drawer and pulled out her Anal Eaze. She squirted some on her hand and put it on the eight-inch strap-on she had put on.

She put the excess on his asshole, sliding her finger inside him once more. "Now open up. Bring 'em back," she said.

Booby did as he was told.

Kim kissed him as she slid the fake dick into him and began pumping. The friction felt good to her, and she fell into it, lifting his legs and fucking him while he lay there panting.

Then she flipped him over and fucked from behind as she thought about how niggas had done her. As she fucked him harder, slapping his ass, he panted and met her beat, spreading his legs open and lifting his ass. Then she reached around and grabbed his dick and began to jack it, sending him crazy.

He flipped back over on his back, and she continued to fuck, and jack his dick, until he screamed, shooting a hot load of semen on her chest and onto her face.

Booby fell back, laid out, trying to catch his breath as she eased the dildo out of his ass. He balled up like a baby, until she laid her warm, cushiony body next to his. When she felt his manhood rise between her legs, she lifted her leg and allowed him to enter.

Booby stroked lazily until he was rock-hard again. Then he pulled out, got on top of her, and he beat her pussy ten times worse than she'd fucked him. When he felt himself about to cum, he pulled out and straddled her, placing his dick between her breasts, and exploded on her neck and chin. He fell over and never moved again, until he was shaken by her the following morning.

"Yo, make sure Joy hit me. You make sure. I needs her large, hefty ass on my team," Booby said, headed out the door. "Hope those nipples on those titties big," he added.

"Shut up, boy," Kim said.

He smiled. "Bet you already know."

"So you think you gonna fuck with me and my girl?"

"Baby, nobody has ever done what we did and never will. That extra shit is between us. You wanted to do it, and I wanted to try it. I like it, but only with a woman. I'll never ever let a nigga touch me. Matter fact, I'll never let another bitch do it. You went where nobody else will ever go. I wouldn't never let nobody know this shit. Muthafuckas might think I'm gay."

"Naw, you just comfortable with yourself, and you a freaky-ass nigga and a nasty-ass man," she said, laughing.

"Naw, I just love y'all fat women. I love y'all. Got this thing for ya. Don't forget me, Kim. Give me some points," he yelled, before getting in his whip pulling off.

Kim laughed. "Fine-ass nigga with a body to kill," she said to herself. "Got the finest bitches on his dick, and all he want is to do all the big hoes."

CHAPTER 9

Kim blew the horn for the second time as she waited on Joy, who finally came out with a serious look on her face.

"What's up, Kim? Good morning to ya. Because mine is fucked up," Joy said as soon as she got in the car.

"What's up, girl?" Kim asked, really wanting to know.

"On the phone arguing with Omari. I guess you can say he my ex. We bought a car. He start going downhill, so I let his ass go. Don't need a nigga bringing me down. I went to Applebee's with a friend of mine. He got mad and took the car. Bitch-ass nigga! I would respect him more if he came home and went to my ass." She smirked, shaking her head.

Kim smirked too. "At least you'll have your car," she joked.

"I appreciate this, Kim, for real."

"No problem, girlfriend. I've been through it all. And I'm still standing. Life ain't a joke. But remember look out for self first, Joy. I got two sons, twenty-two and twenty-four, and I'm thirty-eight. Just bought a new condo three years ago. I've always had it hard, but now I live for me, and Verizon make sure I, I mean we, live good. Fuck him! Go get another car. Let him have the car and take that payment too, you son of a bitch."

Joy laughed, thinking about how the fuck she was gonna get a new car.

"At least you got a couple days to figure things out," Kim said, encouraging her.

"You right. I'll figure it out."

Joy was hoping Minke came through. He had handled mad shit in a fucked up way, but that shit was passed, even though it left scars. But something inside of her always dreamed that he would come back to her.

"Let's go, girl. Snap out of it. I got you after work. Let me know if it change." Kim hit her alarm.

Joy tried her hardest to talk to Omari, but he wasn't trying to hear her. He was really upset about her playing him, and treating him like he was small. No matter what she did or said, it kept coming back to the same shit.

She had finally gotten through her day, when Kim came over.

"So, what's up? Ready?"

"Let's roll," Joy replied as she reached for her ringing phone.

"What's up, ma? What you doing?" the voice said with the strong New York accent.

"Leaving work," she said with a smile.

Kim stared in her face, wondering why she was smiling.

"On my way to Uno's. I'm meeting some of my peoples now. Come on through. I'll meet you up there," Minke said.

"See ya!"

"That was my ex-husband. He wants me to come meet him. We haven't seen each other face to face in years, Kim," Joy said seriously.

"Come on, Joy. Let's get outta here."

They made their way out the building.

"So you want me to drop you off somewhere?" Kim asked as they pulled off.

"Yeah! Uno's. That's much closer anyway."

"Don't matter. I got you. You know Booby want to get with you. That's what he whispered to me last night."

"So why he ain't tell me? I was right there." Joy was wondering why a grown man couldn't speak for himself.

"I don't know. Guess he wanted me to put him in there first."

"Give him my number. See what he talking about. Maybe he'll come give me a dance." Joy smiled.

"That's probably what he trying to do."

They arrived at Uno's and parked in the crowded parking lot.

"What's going on up here?" Kim asked Joy. She dialed Minke's number.

"What up?" Minke answered.

"You here and you gonna carry me home. I got a ride up here, and my girl gotta go," Joy said.

"I'm right here," he said, pulling up. "You see the God, baby?" he asked smiling.

"You in the Lexus?" Joy pointed as she caught a full view of the charcoal grey Lexus.

"Where are you?" he asked, looking around.

"To your right, in the Acura." Joy saw the tinted window come down. Then she saw Sizemo's big smile staring at her, as Minke pulled in the parking space.

"Who's that?" Kim asked.

"That's his man. They like that."

"Good-looking nigga, and he a big boy." Kim smiled.

"And he mad cool. I'll introduce you," Joy said as they got out of the car.

"So what up?" Sizemo yelled, hugging Joy. "And who is this?"

"Kim, this is Sizemo, and this is my husband, Minke," she said, staring at Minke.

"How you?" Minke said to Kim with a nod of the head.

"Damn, Joy! I told you what I wanted and needed in my life, and you went out and found it for me. God, you beautiful," Sizemo said. "Can I hug you too?" He approached Kim with open arms, and she smiled, hugging him back.

"And how are you?" Joy asked Minke.

"I'm fine now," he said as he wrapped his arms around her and squeezed.

Joy hugged him back, thinking he was gonna let go, but he continued to hug her. And the more he squeezed, the more she fell into him, until he was truly holding her up.

He stepped back, touched her face with both hands, and kissed her lips gently, staring into her eyes. "I've been waiting years to say this. I'm sorry. I am so sorry for how I handled things. I can't rewind time and correct my wrong, but I can do right by you now. And I promise, I will. That I will show you."

Minke's eyes watered, but no tears fell. He watched her as tears fell down her face. He didn't have to ask. He knew he'd hurt her deep, and at the time, that was his aim. But over the years, his heart had changed, and he was seeing life differently.

"Thanks, because you never apologize for nothing," Joy said.

"Lecia, I ain't that same dude. Life has taken many turns. I see it different, and I see what's really important," he said, touching her hand and walking toward the entrance of Uno's.

Joy turned to her friend. "What you gonna do, Kim?"

"What you think?" Sizemo said, pulling her with him. "She all right."

They all laughed, walking into Uno's, which was packed. They found a seat and watched the band set up. Minke told them to get some drinks while him and Sizemo met with his employees from the different shops.

As they began to walk off, Joy called Minke.

"What up, babe?"

"I don't have a car, and she picked me up for work. We went out last night, and my friends got me. I don't wanna ask her for nothing else," she said, staring at him.

"Oh! I got that. Order me and Size double Patróns." Minke reached in his pocket and slid her a fifty. "Just hold that. You gonna be all right." He smiled.

"Thanks."

"No need to thank me. I owe you the world," he said and walked off.

Those words brought tears to Joy's eyes again.

Kim saw it, after she sat down. "So that's the nigga," she said, smiling.

"What?"

"You know what I'm talking about, Lecia." Kim laughed. "We all got that nigga in our life. We keep going, we deal with life, but we think about him, and he changes every-thing in your life. He got power to make life great or pull you down to make you feel like shit. Right now, you ain't thinking about Omari and no other nigga. Are you?"

"Nobody. Nobody matters," Joy said with a smile.

"Glad you smiling because you been fucked up all day."

"I ain't fucked up now, I ain't fucked up now," Joy said, her head moving and a big smile.

"So what's with Size? Big, pretty-ass nigga with the pretty hair."

"He real as they come. No-nonsense nigga. I ain't never know him to be all serious. He love to have fun. He mad cool," Joy said, letting her know he was somebody to fuck with.

"Where he from?"

"Think he from here. And if I ain't mistaken, think he from Lake Edward somewhere. Shit! I met him fucking with these Brooklyn niggas, so all I can say is, he about that paper. He run all Minke shit. That's his dude."

"Gotcha, girl," Kim said, picking up her drink, looking over at Size, as she heard the live jazz band begin their session.

Omari had called several times, but Joy ignored his calls. She'd just answered when Kim hit her, letting her know Minke was on his way.

"Gotta go, Omari. Will finish this later. I need my shit." Joy hung up.

Joy stared at Minke as he made his way over to her. He still looked good as hell to her, especially since he had bulked up. *I guess that came from his two-year bid.* He was really filling out his white V-neck, and the True Religion jeans, and blue-and-grey Prada, along with the Prada watch and bracelet, let onlookers know he was that nigga.

As he walked over to the two thickest women, anticipating his company, he glanced over the room to catch all the glances of the attractive women sitting at tables and booths.

"So you all right?" Minke leaned over on the table and made his presence known. "Let me order them something. Then I'll be back." He took one long look at his ex-wife, realizing that she caught and held his attention just like she did years ago. It was hard to break. He just wanted to stare. He shook his head and walked away with his drink.

"Damn!" Joy heard him say as he moved toward the bar.

Sizemo came and stood beside Minke. "So everything good?" he asked.

"No doubt. As long as I'm not coming out of pocket right now. I need for each spot to up its weekly revenue, but we discussed that, so we'll see what happens next week. If it don't change, then I'm gonna make some changes. Like, when I came through today, two of the chairs were empty. I don't give a fuck if them niggas do pay their rent on time, and there every day. I want them at their station all day until you close the door, leave for lunch. If they can't respect that, find a nigga that need that money and don't mind securing his position. I want true moneymakers and go-getters in my shit and around me. This is my life. Niggas don't know."

"Feel you, bossman," Sizemo said, knowing Minke didn't play when it came to these businesses.

"So what's with mommy, son?" Minke asked.

"She seem chill. Just talkin' for a second. She act like she with it. You know me. Love to hit a big one every now and then." Sizemo was serious.

"You can have 'em, son. Fuckin with those hoes is a lot of work. Lecia wa'n't never that big, but I fell in love with her when she was small, so that love still there. It didn't and don't matter. I'll always have love for her, and she's my kids' mother. But now that I'm older and been through all these phat-ass, big-tittie, thick black bitches, my choices are a little different, preferably a little smaller. That's what turn me on. And they ain't got to be black."

"You done with black hoes, son?" Sizemo smiled.

"I ain't done, but right now what turn me on is that exotic shit wit' tight bodies, like my Dominican thing up top, or my shit I fuck wit' in D.C. Know what I mean? Do you hear me, son?"

"Yeah, I hear ya. But I love these black shorties and I love to fuck a fat girl from time to time, especially a pretty one." Sizemo began making his way to the table, with Minke right behind him.

After a few drinks and light conversation, they decided to make moves. Kim carried Sizemo back to his truck that he'd left in front of the shop, and Minke took Joy to her spot.

"So how long you been living here?" Minke asked, as they entered the little apartment.

"I guess for a couple years. I had to get something I could afford. I been out here fucked up for so long and been without, I don't care if I have to have muthafuckas sleeping on the floor or in the tub. I'll never be fucked up again." Joy looked at Minke with a serious attitude, so he'd know she wasn't joking or playing in no way.

"I feel you, Lecia. You always been stronger than you gave yourself credit for, I knew you would come to see that in your own time." Minke walked over to the counter, where he pulled out some weed and a fresh Dutch.

"So where the kids? What they been doing?" he asked, looking around the apartment then walking in her room.

"Probably in the room."

Minke finished rolling his Dutch and lit it.

Just then, his son walked out the room. "Ma, where you been? You usually don't come in here this late. Where you been?"

"Don't question my woman. She been with me. Is that okay?" Minke said, startling his son.

"Dad!" Juan yelled as he ran in his father's arms, almost making him drop his Dutch.

Minke wrapped his arms around his son and held him almost as tight as he was holding him.

Lecia walked to her doorway and stood staring at her two men. She didn't know what she was feeling. Her heart was in her stomach.

And the ringing of her phone made the feeling worse. Minke had left her hanging dry, and for all the men she'd pass time with her business, not his. And she didn't need for him to know anything she'd done or how she was living. She wanted him to look at her as that woman, like he did before that shit got in his head. She didn't want him to think she had changed in a negative way. So she ignored her phone, with plans to turn it off as soon as she got the opportunity.

"Your sister 'sleep?" Minke asked, with little expression.

"Yes, come in here. She always knocked out." Juan guided his dad to their room.

Minke looked at his daughter then leaned down and gave her a kiss.

She turned slowly, flipping over, realizing she'd been disturbed. She tried to focus on the man she hadn't seen in years. "Daddy," she said in a slur, wiping her eyes.

"You okay, baby girl? Go back to sleep. I'll be here when you get up." He smiled at her and kissed her again.

"You staying here with us, Dad?" Juan asked.

"Me and your mom been talking, son, you know, trying to catch up, but I can say that I'm not going far ever again. That you believe, okay," Minke said, looking into his son's eyes. "You two get some rest, and we'll talk later," he added and walked back into the front room.

Minke flipped on the TV and sat down. He lit his el again.

Joy was in the bathroom with the door shut, but he couldn't help but hear her on the phone telling someone she would call them back when she finished taking her shower. And a shot of jealousy ran through him.

He got back up and made his way to her bedroom. They hadn't been together in years, and he knew she hadn't been alone. But looking at how she was living, he figured, if she had a man in her life, working at Verizon, she should have a little more than she did.

He looked around at the old apartment and thought about the location. It was in one of the slummiest areas of town, with dirty, pissy hallways, and niggas hanging all out in the front. And she had two old-ass TVs, and the furniture looked as if it came with the place, secondhand for sure. The only thing that looked new was the bedroom set.

He heard her come out the shower while he was flipping through the stations.

Joy appeared in the doorway wearing her short pink terry cloth dress that she'd turned into a nightie after it got old. It was revealing a lot of skin.

Minke couldn't see her big ass wearing that in the street, but what? He didn't really know her anymore. "You hitting this?" He held out the el for her to grab.

"Hell, yeah," she answered and sat down beside him. "Smell like some good-good." She took the smoke and inhaled like she was hitting a joint.

"Kush, baby. You ain't got to hit it like you hitting some bullshit. That ain't nothing but the truth." Minke smiled. "So where you moving to?" he asked, sitting on the edge of the couch.

For some reason, Minke didn't feel comfortable. This hood shit wasn't really him anymore. He liked being in nice shit, in a nice area, but he tried to understand that she was doing the best she could. He was glad she was moving, especially since he was going to be hanging around.

Her phone rang again, and she ignored it. Then it rang again. That's when he realized why he had this uncomfortable feeling.

"Give me a second." She passed him the Dutch and went in the room to answer her phone.

"I'll be right back. Running to the Smoke Shack I saw up the street," he said, looking at her backside. "Need anything?"

"What you going to get?" she asked. Joy could see something in his eyes change every time her phone rang.

"Box of Dutches and a pack of Newports. Might stop and get some beer."

"Naw, I'm good," she said, picking up the phone as Minke walked out.

"Who you talking to?" Omari asked.

"What you want? We got something to talk about. My car. So if that ain't the conversation, then again, what do you want?"

"Who you comin' off like that on? I wanna sit down and talk and you trying to be funny," Omari said angrily.

"Son, you are stressing me. If you not here to bring me up, which you ain't, then leave me alone. Omari, please. I got to get shit together." She listened to him go on and on about nothing, until she heard the knock at the door. "I gotta go, boy. Later."

"I heard that knock. Who is that?" he yelled before he heard the phone go dead, sending a burst of rage and jealousy through him.

Joy opened the door and turned her phone on vibrate.

Minke walked inside, catching a funny feeling when he saw her step outside the apartment door and lock the main door to the apartment building.

He rolled another Dutch and grabbed a Heineken before he sat back down next to her. "So, Alecia, I know life's been a struggle, but talk to me. How you been? What you been up to?"

"Nothing. Just going to work and coming home. I don't really do nothing," she answered. But she knew he wanted more, he never said her whole name unless something was on his mind and he was serious.

Minke pulled on the Dutch real hard and blew it out. He took a long, hard gulp of his Heineken and was getting ready to say something when her phone began to vibrate again, back to back. He didn't feel like he had the right to really say anything, seeing he was just coming back into her life.

"You do more than go to work and come home. You got some other shit cracking, the way that phone keep going off. And it's after eleven."

Joy sat quiet for a second then she finally spoke.

"I had a friend, but it didn't work. He was real jealous, and every time he thought some shit, I went through hell proving otherwise. That day I went and saw Size, we went to eat at Applebee's. Somehow he found out, and the next day, he took my car."

Minke smirked. "How he take your car?"

"He helped me with the down payment, and I had it in his name because my license was messed up. So he came and took it."

"So y'all were serious?"

"Not like that. He was a close friend," she said, getting more frustrated with the conversation.

"Did he live with you and my kids?" he asked, looking at her. "Were y'all together like that?"

"He stayed here sometimes."

"So he had a key to your house and car?" Minke's heart was crushed. It had been a while, but he could never picture her being with another dude.

"Look, girls use that friend shit like it's nothing. But if you living with a dude, sharing the same bed every night, fucking a nigga day in and day out, guess what? He's not a friend, he's your man. And if he feel like that, then his feelings make him act in a jealous, protective way. And you as a woman can't do shit to control him. That's why I asked you, 'What's up?' Please don't have me in no shit."

"I'm not with noboby, and I don't have a man, so I don't need to hear all that." Her phone began to vibrate again.

"Answer that. Whoever trying to get in touch with you, if they know where you live, you rather talk to them and let them know the deal. You don't want them coming around, wilding out."

"Nobody better not come over here wilding. This is my spot and—"

Bam! Bam! Bam!

Suddenly, they heard banging at the front door.

Minke smirked at her while she sat still as if things changed to slow motion.

Seconds later the banging came to her living room window, while the yelling of her name let her know that Omari was outside and wasn't going away. She looked at Minke, with her eyes wide.

He could see she was scared and had been caught up in a situation that wasn't good. "Go outside, baby. Get your dude. Talk to him, before I have to put the spark to him." Minke smirked. "Brooklyn, baby. My nigga Big already warned niggas," he said with a serious look and a calm tone. "Maybe he ain't heard."

Then they heard and saw the window shatter. They both jumped up, and by the time Minke got to his feet, the 9 mm Beretta was in his hand.

"No, Minke, please!" Joy yelled as her kids came out the room.

When she saw Minke cock the gun and put one in the chamber, she exited the house and went out front, yelling, "What is wrong with you, Omari? Go home!"

"I am home, bitch! Fuck is you doing, locking the door? You got a nigga in my shit?" he said, trying to make his way in.

"You can't come in my house, Omari!" she yelled, grabbing his arm. But she instantly felt his hands wrap around her neck, lift her on her toes, and guide her inside.

"That's Omari, Dad," Juan said. "He's a big dude."

"Go in the room."

Boom!

The door flew open, and Joy's body landed on the floor.

But the butt of the 9 mm against Omari's head dropped him to his knees. When he looked up, the barrel of the 9 mm brought him back to his senses. He stayed on his knees, not being able to move, his life flashing before him.

"Wrong house, wrong girl, wrong night. This is my wife and kids, my dude," Minke said, his finger on the trigger.

Joy lay on the floor speechless, tears in her eyes, her hands over her mouth.

"Don't shoot Omari, Daddy. He's nice. He plays with me," Minke heard his daughter say, and it weakened him. He couldn't pull the trigger.

"Go! Get out!" Joy screamed at the top of her lungs.

Omari crawled out the door, jumped to his feet, and burst.

Joy looked at Minke, and in his eyes all she saw was murder, that same look she had seen before in his eyes and Hitler's. He was looking straight through her.

She got to her feet and walked over, put her arms around her kids, and went into the room, shaking.

Minke walked outside to see Omari flying out the parking lot. He came inside and shut the door, sat the 9mm on the table, and lit his Dutch.

"Damn, Hitler! Why niggas want me outta here, either locked or earthed, cousin? You always said, 'Drugs, money, and bitches, one of them always get a nigga.' I've done good with the drugs and the money, but these bitches, oh, my God! Only you can protect me," he said in a low tone, trying to calm down. His adrenaline was running high, but he'd learned to stay calm, stay alert, and stay on point.

"Alecia!" he yelled. "Alecia, get the fuck out here, man!"

Still scared, she came out moving slow, her neck bruised and tears in her eyes.

"Got any more fuckin' friends? Huh? Let's deal with all this shit tonight."

"No," she said softly.

"Here," he said, passing her the Dutch. "Take that in the room and get dressed. I don't wanna stay here."

"Juan!" he yelled. "Get dressed and put something on your sister. We out."

In minutes they were dressed and in the Lex, rolling downtown, where Minke got a suite at the Marriott Waterside.

Juan and Quandra ran and dove into the twin beds, while Lecia ran the water to the Jacuzzi tub, so she could take a bath and relax her mind, which was still racing.

Minke rolled up another Dutch and walked into his kids' room. "We all right?"

"Yes, Daddy. I like this," Quandra said, smiling.

"Glad you do, baby. Get some sleep." Minke looked over at his son, who had a smile, and was shaking his head. "What's that look for, cuz?"

"Nothing. I thought I was gonna have to pull Omari off ya," Juan joked.

"Understand, son, you can't stop no man from jumping on ya, because that's his choice. But you better be able to get any man off ya, by any means necessary. Don't ever let nobody hurt you, got me? Maybe my way ain't the best way, but it works." Minke smiled. "Love ya," he said, closing their door.

Minke walked back into the master suite to find Lecia soaking and handed her the Dutch. After kicking off his shoes, he grabbed a washcloth, leaned beside the tub, and began to bathe her.

Joy closed her eyes as he gently took the rag across her breasts, floating on the water. He continued, until she almost dozed off because of the relaxed state he had put her body in.

He grabbed a towel and wrapped around her as she stepped out and continued to dry her. He guided her to the bed and laid her down and began to massage her body from head to toe. Joy fell asleep to his soothing touch.

The days that followed made Joy feel as if the last several years of her life was a bad dream.

She woke to the poking of Minke's thick, 9-inch dick on her leg. *He didn't even do anything last night,* she thought. She looked down and saw the gap in his boxers, and wondered if she should take him there, after all that happened last night. *All right,* she thought.

She eased down, reached in his fly, and helped release his manhood. Minke jumped, but before he could respond, she was giving him full, wet kisses on his head.

Minke felt something inside him that made him relax, but when her wet, warm mouth eased down on him slowly, his legs tightened. He took a deep breath, as she gave him the greatest morning head he'd ever had.

Joy felt the pre-cum leaking into her mouth. She knew he was about to cum, but before she could make a decision, he made it for her and allowed his juices to shoot down her throat. Joy kept going and swallowed every drop, until he eased back, trying to catch his breath.

She got up and walked in the bathroom, and he heard her gargling and spitting, before she returned to say, "Good morning."

"Great morning," he said with a smile. "So what you gotta pay to get your license?"

"What?" she asked, wondering where that came from.

"You know me, and you know I got shit to do. Now I'm trying to get us situated before I go anywhere. Now answer the question," he said sternly.

"Five hundred dollars, Monday. My insurance fee lapsed, and they got me. And I got to show an SR-22 with insurance, and I can get my license."

"You get on the phone and see what insurance company is open today, so you can get the SR-22. We gonna order breakfast, you run to DMV, pay the fees. By the time you come back, we'll go to the mall and get the day going. Go ahead because we got a lot to get done, and time ain't on our side." Minke gave her money to pay her fines.

Three hours later she came in smiling with her license in hand.

Minke asked to see the house they were moving to, so they got in the car and drove to the new town house out Lake Edward. Lecia called the owner to see if they could meet her, so her family could see the place. After looking through it they stood in the living room smiling.

Juan and Quandra were overjoyed at the thought of having their own rooms, so they were all taken by surprise when Minke asked the owner what they would need for Lecia to get the key today.

The owner said, "If you have the security deposit and first month's rent, I would ignore the last couple days of the present month."

Minke sent Joy to the car and told her to look in the armrest then go to the 7-Eleven and get money orders.

Alecia returned again smiling. It was done. Then they went from the house to Grand Furniture, and back to the hotel.

Sunday came and Lecia had to go to church to give all praise to God, and to her surprise again, Minke joined her.

After church, they rode by the house of one of his close friends in Buckner Farms. He had several cars in his driveway and yard that he'd purchased at the auction.

Lecia left driving her own new Honda Accord. This was not real. Minke had spent an abundance of money. Nothing to him, but everything to her. She had her life back, and he was catering to his woman.

Monday morning Joy walked into work with a glow. She couldn't do anything but smile. Kim was the first one to call her on it, and Joy told her she would talk to her at lunch.

When lunchtime came, she couldn't wait to talk to Kim, but to her surprise, Kim already knew what went down. She happened to be with Sizemo when Minke called him about the incident. What she didn't know was, Omari had been calling her all morning, and that she finally got annoyed with him blowing up her phone, and answered to tell him not to call her anymore.

But Omari was trying to keep calm. All he wanted to know was, when he could return her car, and was Minke still there. She let him know that Minke was no longer there, leaving out that she wasn't either, and that he could keep the car, and that she thought it would be best if he didn't call or come around anymore.

Kim listened to Joy release all her drama with much anguish. Then she saw how her mood changed when she switched the subject to Minke. She had been blessed that his heart had changed, that the man she knew was back in her life. Kim could see the happiness in Joy's eyes. Her friend was gonna be okay.

CHAPTER 10

For the next several weeks, Joy was on cloud nine. She had her family back, and Minke was looking at her as if he could eat her up. His actions showed his love, and his love showed his commitment. And she gave her all to the man who was there for her in every way and continued to comfort him with her body. He treated it so well, each and every time they made love, it showed.

With Minke there were no barriers. He went all out, but he noticed the experience Alecia had gained in their years apart. He chalked it up to her missing him, letting herself go, and not caring about anybody and anything outside of them.

Then one day she was at work and got a picture text from him. She got excited because she had gotten used to him sending sweet texts daily, and even pictures of himself smiling, expressing his love, and how happy he was at this time in his life. But today her smile was washed away, and her heart dropped when she retrieved the pictures.

First it was a picture of a packed box. She instantly noticed it was the box she had in the hall closet with several boxes on top of it. She never thought he would ever go in it. Since the first couple weeks of them moving in, Minke was gone for days at a time then home for a week or two, and when he wasn't home, he was in the street, handling business.

The thought never entered her mind that he would ever go through her stuff. He wasn't that type of dude. But the next picture she got proved her wrong. He had laid her photo album on the bed, the album she had with all the pictures of them in the beginning, and all the pictures of each dude she'd fucked with while they were apart. She saw her camera that she'd allowed guys to take pictures of her in her different negligees, which she'd packed in the same box along with the toys. She saw the picture of the towel in which she'd wrapped her silver bullet, electric tongue, black twelve-inch dildo, and the liquid Anal Eaze. She sat staring at the picture knowing he was gonna paint a picture that he had never had in his head.

Now what is he thinking? she thought.

She got up and walked out with a turning stomach and teary eyes. She dialed his number, ready to hear some shit.

"Hello," he answered.

"What's going on, Minke?"

"You tell me. I need to know who I'm fucking with. If you've changed like that, I just wanna know who I'm fucking with."

"I've dated since you; you wa'n't there. I was single, and all those toys belong to my roommate I had when I first got the place. We talked about Tam. I told you she was out there. She liked anal sex and a lot of other shit. I should have thrown it all away, but I knew I would return it to her sooner or later."

"I understand we weren't together. But did you feel so low about yourself that you let all those nothing-ass niggas fuck? Damn! I showed you from the beginning what you were worth. And I gave you the world. Yeah, all the bullshit we went through fucked us up, but I thought I showed you your worth."

"They were just friends. I didn't fuck them. We just hung out, talked shit, and played cards."

"I hear ya, baby. Go ahead and get back to work. We'll talk later. You okay?"

Joy heard the disappointment in his voice. She just wanted to get to him and show him that she loved him and that the love she had in her, and all the love she had to give, was for him and him alone.

Later on that night, as Joy was fixing dinner, she could sense the tension in the air between her and Minke. She was determined to make things right.

"Baby, I just want you to trust me and know that all the love I have is for you, and I just want you to give me the chance to prove that to you in any way I can," she pleaded as she wrapped her arms around his neck.

Minke ducked her advances. He wanted to believe her, but deep down inside, he just couldn't shake the images of what he had seen. And thoughts of her giving her body to all of those men turned his stomach in knots.

Over the next several months, Joy gave her all, but she could see and feel the distance growing. Lately, when he came in town, all he had was weed and dick, and most of the time it was just weed, since his interest in making love to her was slowly decreasing.

One night while laying in bed she asked if he was losing his interest, and it took him a long time to answer.

Minke let her know that, since he saw those pictures and toys, he looked at her in a different way. He wasn't proud to be with her and felt funny when they were together, knowing mad niggas had been with her. That didn't make him feel special. And if the thought came to his mind, which it didn't often, he wasn't turned on, and if he pushed the thought out of his mind, it would work. But if it came back while they were making love, his dick would instantly go soft.

He went on to explain that he had to think of other shit, other bitches, anything to keep him hard. Making love went out the window. He had to feel like she wasn't shit, that she was just some nasty, fat bitch with big-ass titties that he was just stopping through, fucking with.

That's why he started fucking on the couch, in the kitchen, on the side of the bed. he would just drop his jeans and fuck, so it would feel like freak shit, so he could hurry and get a nut before his dick went soft. He loved her, but she didn't do it for him anymore, and he had finally realized that he didn't want her. But he still didn't want her to be with no one else. And being the man he was, he knew that wasn't fair to her or him. And, plus, he was tired of trying so hard.

Minke came around a few more times, but his visits became shorter. Then she would hear he was in town, but he didn't come to her house.

When she confronted him about it, he let her know that he was done. Then he left her town house, took all his shit, and left her key.

Joy was devastated. She felt as if her life wasn't shit again. She felt so low, but she knew she had given her all. She hated him for coming back into her life and bringing up all those old feelings then leaving her again, but she respected him because of his commitment to his kids. He didn't leave her fucked up. He told her, no matter what, he was gonna continue to hold her down because she had his kids. And he never stopped.

Joy kept her hopes rolling for months that he would change his mind, but she just kept hearing stories from Kim, Malaina, and Lady about him being in town, ballin' out with different bitches.

The crushing blow was when her son came home from spending a couple days with his dad and told her about the new house he had bought for his new twenty-year-old stepmom and his new little brother. Joy was floored, but it was the eye-opener she needed. She had to move on. She knew he didn't want her anymore for sure.

CHAPTER 11

Joy got back in church, and started feeling like she had the strength to move on. Then Minke began calling, but she couldn't find the strength to tell him no, just like she couldn't tell him about her other side.

She knew he would come with some shit, and he did. And she allowed him to dictate her life and moves. He would stop by the house whenever, which was fine at first, but once she heard he was living with his baby momma, then that was deaded. But it never stopped.

One night while out with the girls at the new, improved club, Broadway, they stood by the bar sipping their drinks, and were startled by the ruckus as some dudes came their way.

"What up, ladies?" the guy said, his hat pulled low.

The girls stared, until Kim yelled, "Booby!"

They hugged him, and when he smiled at Malaina and Joy, they remembered him. As he hugged them, his boys walked off. Then he hugged Joy, holding her tight and looking her in the eyes.

"What you staring at?" she asked, a confused look on her face.

"You. Can I call you later?" He handed her his Black-Berry.

She put her number in and handed it back. He smiled, and inside she melted. She really felt something when he smiled at her.

Later they talked and indulged in some really deep conversation. Booby actually listened to her and tried his hardest to understand who she was and where she was coming from, without judging her. Booby became her friend.

She remembered the night he ended up in her bed. It was Valentine's Day. She was thinking it was another fucked up day. Minke had called and sent flowers to the job, but it was a week he didn't shit on her. She was beginning to allow his slanders to bounce off her, but sometimes he came hard, making her feel she really wasn't shit.

But even though Booby was just her friend, he showed love like she was his only woman, making her feel special. And when he showed up Valentine's Day with roses, a tennis bracelet, and that sexy smile, she greeted him like never before.

She excused herself and returned in a short red silk nightgown with matching robe. He attacked her, kissing her neck then sucking and licking. He slid his hand and gripped her love lips and massaged them lightly in his four fingers, until her wetness came slipping through.

Booby threw a finger in her, and she relaxed. Then he threw another and gripped the upper part of her vagina and began massaging her insides. Her head relaxed back, her lips parted lightly, Joy licked her lips as her love muscles squeezed his fingers.

Booby got up slowly and took off his clothes. He watched her move her hands down to her vagina and massage her clit. He had a fire burning inside of her.

He wasted no time getting on her, no condom. She was gonna say no, but he was already inside her, damaging her. All she could do was open up and accept him, and Booby took his time serving her.

Then he pulled out and came on her stomach, grabbed a towel, wiped himself off, then wiped her stomach. And he was back inside of her, pumping steadily as his body heated, but she surprised him, by coming back with his every thrust.

Her body got wetter and wetter, and he was ready to cum, so he went under her knees, to her shoulders, and pulled her legs up. Joy was now balled up, two huge breasts with large circles and small, hardened nipples staring at him. He looked down into her pretty face and stared at her lying there with her eyes closed, her small lips parted, the sounds of warm, gushing womanhood sucking him in. He relaxed and allowed all his weight to fall into her soft thighs, stomach, and breasts.

Joy wrapped her big arms around him, and he melted into her and began to cum. She squeezed him every way possible, to drain him dry. He rolled over off in a fetal position, and she never let him go. And that was the best sleep they had in a long time.

Their time spent together increased, and the sex made time pass like no other.

But Joy couldn't shake Minke. Booby made her feel so good, but afterwards, Minke would come to mind, and she'd be there in body only.

After a few weeks, things began to slow down. She realized Booby was a great fuck, that he had caught her in a down mode and lifted her, which she mistook for more than it was. But as these feelings came flowing down, Booby disappeared, and Joy was hurt.

Then she found out he had gotten locked up on a concealed weapons charge and possession. She was floored when she got the news from Kim.

"I knew he did more than dance," Joy said. "I told his ass to be careful."

"Girl, he was doing his thing. He wa'n't even dancing no more," Kim said.

"Don't I know. He carried his own, but he wa'n't scared to ask for some change." Joy laughed, only to keep from crying. He was her friend and he'd been there to lean on, and he knew how to carry it.

"Booby's a good guy. Hope he gonna be okay."

"He's gonna be okay. I got that nigga. He showed me how a real friend gets down. That's my dude," Joy said, thinking of how she was gonna handle shit with him.

CHAPTER 12

"What the fuck! You sitting around looking all fucked up," Minke said, walking into Joy's house.

"Tired. Tired of just working and coming home. I'm tired of being by myself," she said.

"Chill, son. That's why I gave you kids. You always got something to do." Minke started laughing.

"Not funny. I'm serious."

"Find a hobby. Work out with me." He passed her the lit Dutch.

"Fuck that! I'm fine." She pulled on the Dutch.

"Well, get right. Let's roll out and do something," he said, realizing she was going through something at that time.

He hadn't been there for her like in the beginning. He was doing all he could to push her away, but at the same time, not allowing her to go too far, because his heart couldn't stand it. But he tried to look at her as his sweet, adorable Lecia.

She wasn't there for him like before. She didn't answer his every call. If he came by late, she might be home, or she might not be, but she always came up with some shit. She never told him she was with the next dude, even though he knew. But it was something he buried, convincing himself she was just a fuck. A cool friend he could smoke, drink, and talk with, and fuck whenever and however he wanted.

She never stopped telling him she loved him, she never stopped asking him to marry her again, and she never told him no, no matter what he asked, and always made him feel he was her only one whenever they spoke or were together. So Minke began to take it all as a game in his head.

"So where we going?"

"Let's go out to Ghent. Grab a bite and talk," he said, heading out the door.

They jumped in the Lexus and made their way out to Colley Avenue to the bar and lounge.

"So what up with you, Lecia?" Minke asked, putting quarters in the pool table.

"What you mean, Minke?" Alecia reached for two pool sticks then picked up the menu.

"All this missing time, not answering your phone. I come by at night, you ain't home, and you don't pick up, and when you do call me back, you on some bullshit. What the fuck you think I'm talking about?" Minke stepped closer, looking at her then the menu. "Fuck you getting?"

"I don't know. Chicken fingers and fries. You get the buffalo shrimp, so I can try it." She got the waitress' attention and made the order. She also ordered their drinks.

Minke liked the fact she handled that shit and she knew him so well, it made him comfortable.

"Talk to me, Lecia." He cracked the balls.

"Minke, I hang out to keep from being so bored. All I do is work. I got friends, and we just hang out."

"You must be fucking with them like that. You can't answer yo' shit."

"It ain't like that. We talk shit, hang out, play cards, but that is it."

"You over niggas house after twelve, and they ain't asking for no pussy? You got me fucked up." Minke looked at her.

"It ain't like that, Minke. And you ain't there. Oh! I forgot. You got some other shit in town, with a new bitch staying with you, and you coming at me? Nigga, please. You never answer yo shit. I mean, never. I never know when you in town. Don't get me wrong. I know you got to make your moves back home and shit, but you said it was me and you, Minke," she said, moving closer to him.

"Don't I got you? Aren't you good?"

"Minke, you were my husband. You always took care of things with money. But I'm lonely. I want somebody to come home to, somebody to go out with, somebody to talk to in the evening and then hold me. I know what that feels like. A man don't have to have shit, but if he coming with all that, then it's hard not to try to love him."

Minke stared at her, feeling her every word, and reached out and took her into his arms.

"I hear you, Lecia. Baby, I'm here, and I'm gonna be here for ya. I love you."

"I love you too, Minke," she said, looking at him.

Joy loved him to no end, but he was on another level in the game right now, and he was making money. But he had allowed these bitches to start playing roles and holding shit, and that was a dangerous game, especially when he started fucking them. She tried to believe him, and even though she knew he was fucking up, she always opened her arms and showed him love and allowed her guard to come down.

Minke knew what he was capable of and where to change his game. He catered to her need for attention, her need to be wanted, her need to be shown that she belonged, and again he was back in their house enjoying his woman again.

Her need to want love that bad made her cling to him and bow down to his every need and want, knowing he needed to be loved, that he needed to know that she wanted him in every way. And even though he had a bitch in a crib waiting, she allowed him to make his way into her bed and give her the best love she'd ever had, and in return she gave the best love she'd ever given.

And she felt she was in heaven again, for four days. Then he began the same shit—not answering his phone, not calling for days. Then he would pop up claiming he missed her so bad, and he needed to feel her. And he'd pull her in the room and fuck hard for about twenty minutes and be gone in thirty, leaving no evidence that he was ever there, except for the wet rag in the bathroom, her wet ass, and a hurt heart.

She could never tell him no, no matter how he made her feel, good or bad. And this became their relationship. But anytime Joy was out or had company, she would hear some of the most degrading things come out of Minke's mouth, making her feel lower than dirt. He would leave her sitting in the house by herself, feeling like nothing.

Joy sat at the bar beside Lady. They had decided to meet at the Roger Brown's, one of the new sports bars opened by an ex-NFL player in downtown Portsmouth. Joy wasn't pressed to go, but Lady assured her it was an event to not miss. Kim was supposed to meet them also, but hadn't arrived.

"Where Malaina? She coming out?" Lady sipped on her Goose and Malibu, her chill-out drink.

"She with her jump-off. Told her she better slow down. That nigga ain't got shit to offer her if her husband find out." Joy said.

"That's where these hoes fuck up, fucking with these broke-ass niggas. Don't fuck with shit less than your man," Lady said, "not even for no dick. Every nigga gots to have potential."

They both laughed.

"I just need me a man for some dick, conversation, attention. Shit, I don't care if he curses me out from time to time, but just don't curse me out and leave." Joy shook her head. "Stay there and fuss then let's make up."

"You talking about one person. You messed up because you allowed Minke to come in your life. No, come back into your life and turn it upside down. You were doing fine. Yeah, I can tell that's your boo, and every bitch got that dude who does something to them and they just can't resist. But sooner or later, you as a woman got to realize what's good for you."

"Ain't that right," Kim said, catching the tail end of the conversation. Looking fly as ever, she hugged Joy and Lady.

"What up, girl?" Joy smiled, glad to see her friend.

"Damn, Kim! That shit hot!" Lady said, admiring Kim's pants suit.

"Came out tonight on some business shit. I want a nigga talking about money, not ass tonight."

"Can't hide those titties," Lady said. "Don't even try it."

They all laughed.

"Order me an appletini. I got to go pee," Kim said, walking off.

"You heard what I said, didn't you, Joy?" Lady asked. "I'm tired of you crying and being down. "

"I know, but I feel like he gonna come around. We've been through too much."

"Yeah, but you gave him every opportunity to come in and love you and be there. He takes advantage of the situation. He's not there for you, except on the money tip, and he gonna continue because of his kids. And if he not, you doing it now, he got you up. Now stay the fuck up," Lady said directly, as if she had no more to say.

"You right. But I was trying my hardest to pull my family back together. It was my fault our shit got fucked up."

"Look at me," Lady said, staring at Joy. "No, the lifestyle fucked it up. How he lived, how his cousin lived, and the shit that came with street life is what caused your life to go the way it did. Sooner or later your views change, you change, and then your life gonna change."

"Believe me, I'm starting to realize and know what I want and what I need," Joy said with a crooked smile.

"Do your thing. Get a smile on that beautiful face. You deserve it."

Kim came back. "So what's going on? This is all right. I never come on this side." She stared at her girls. "Why y'all so serious in the club?"

"No seriousness," Lady said. "Just girl talk."

"Must be talking about men and how they be fuckin' up. A subject that can go on forever, a nonstop conversation."

As the conversation continued, two men in suits approached Lady.

"Hello," one of the guys said. "Can I have a dance?"

"I don't dance. I only two-step," the other guy said, looking at Kim. "But I'll dance with you,"

"Naw, I'm all right," Kim said.

Both of them burst out laughing.

"What's up, Lady? What the hell you been up to?"

"Nothing. Holding down the shop. Making sure this money don't stop," Lady replied. "What up with y'all? And where the fuck is y'all third wheel? Oooh, my bad. Kim, Joy, this Quan and Dwayne. I grew up with these cats," she said, introducing her friends.

Kim and Joy had no interest in the suit-wearing dudes, so they indulged in their own conversation.

Then another guy came in the door, headed straight toward them. Not saying a word to Kim and Joy, he went straight to Lady. The conversation was short and serious. He stared at the dudes talking to Lady, and they eased away.

Kim and Joy wondered who the dude was with the all-black Prada. They could tell he had money, from the tight European-style clothes he wore, to the Rolex on his arm and the two diamond studs.

"Who you with? I'm ready to chill," he said to Lady in a low voice, but Joy and Kim overheard him.

"I'm with my girls. Joy, Kim, this is Manolo," she said loud enough for him to recognize her introduction.

"They on your team?" he asked.

"Yeah! Not like that though," Lady said.

"Well, what's up? Let me get a drink. Then I'm outta here. You got me?" Manolo looked Lady in the face.

"Got you, nigga. Holla when you ready," she said, and Manolo walked off.

"What he mean, 'on your team'?" Joy asked.

"Naw, he got dough . . . real dough. And he like to parley with girls, and I hold him down. I know girls who waiting to get down and make money."

"For real?" Kim asked. "You get money too?"

"Yeah, just for setting them up."

"And you don't get down?" Joy asked.

"Not usually, but if I do, you better believe that they pay like they weigh. That's some other shit though."

Joy and Kim looked at each other surprised. They knew Lady was about her work, but never knew to what extent.

Moments later they saw Manolo look at Lady and head toward the door. Then Lady said her good-byes, gave them hugs, and she was out the door.

Joy and Kim sat at the bar getting nice, both wondering exactly what Lady was up to. They knew she was about her business, but never did they figure she was selling herself or selling the girls in her clique.

The colorful eye shadow, the false lashes, the flawless foundation, and Barbie doll-painted lips, all the revealing gear, the upgrades that really made men look at you started to come into focus, when Kim said it.

"Is your girl selling pussy?"

"I don't know, but that's not my steez," Joy said.

"Well, that's how dude came off," Kim said. "Like that money rule her."

"You're right. I'm thinking the same thing." *I don't want to be known as a bitch that chase money, but I don't wanna be out here and niggas think I'm selling pussy*, Joy thought. She never wanted nothing like that to get to Minke.

"So what's up, girl? This shit ain't really hittin' to me. These niggas ain't truly ballin' and coming at a bitch tonight," Kim said.

"Maybe they don't like fat hoes." Joy chuckled.

"Shit! What nigga don't want a big diva? The problem is keeping the nigga, because they always want to shine with a perfect ten, nice slamming body, and cute face. But when it come to sex, we know and they know that they want something to grab onto. You know you ain't never had no problem getting a man. It's just keeping him."

"You right. Unless you find a fine-ass nigga like Booby who love a big girl. He used to just lay around and rub me, just rub all over me, and he made me feel so comfortable," Joy said sadly, the alcohol fucking with her.

"Don't start, girl," Kim said. "He'll be home soon enough."

Kim was hoping in the back of her mind that Booby's time went fast, because that was her nigga too, and what they shared was unheard of. She didn't realize how close she had gotten to Booby and had started catching feelings from their little sexcapade. She was a woman with a lot of freak in her, and the only man who allowed her to do whatever she wanted was Booby, a man so comfortable with his manhood and with himself that he let her show him how good other things could feel. If it was freakish, he wanted to try it. If she said she'd seen it or heard that it felt good, he was down.

They both sat sipping on their drinks, looking around the club at the scenery, with the same man on their mind.

Joy started thinking about how he was a beast in the bed, and how the nigga slung dick like a porno star, keeping her body soaking wet as he fucked the hell out of her. As the thoughts ran through her mind, her body began to moisten. This was one night she wished Minke would call.

She picked up the phone and dialed him, but no answer. After several attempts, her calls still went unanswered. "Damn! I can't even get no dick. Bitch need that tonight," she said, looking through her phone.

"Know what you mean. I'm gonna call my old faith-ful." Kim pulled out her phone.

"Who you calling, Kim?"

"Yo boy, big Sizemo."

"I ain't know you was still seeing him," Joy said, with a speck of jealousy and not knowing why.

"Yeah, he finally came clean about his girl, but we still hook up. That big muthafucka will come through, eat this pussy, then bang it up and put my ass to sleep, and he be gone. We both know what it is, and it works. I just got to keep my feelings in order because he that nigga that will get your ass caught up if you not care-ful." Kim smiled.

Kim thought she was telling Joy something she didn't know, but Joy had seen Sizemo run girls crazy. He was the cool-ass, down-to-earth nigga that girls had no prob-lem feeling, but knew what time it was.

Kim sat on the phone for a few, and Joy watched as smiles kept coming across her face as if she was the happiest girl in the club.

"Fuck you keep smiling for? That nigga ain't sayin' shit," Joy said, knowing Sizemo could overhear her.

Kim laughed. "Don't be mad because my dude whis-pering sweet nothings in my ear."

"Sweet nothings, exactly," Joy said, getting close to Kim's phone to make sure Sizemo could hear her. "That fat-ass nigga ain't saying nothing. Not a god-damn thing."

"Tell her she better shut the hell up before I tell my man to go at her ass for getting out of line and sticking her nose in grown folk business." Sizemo laughed.

Kim told her what he said, and they all had a laugh.

"Better tell him to come handle his fuckin' business. Shit! A bitch in need over here." Joy said with a smirk, but serious as they come. Then she heard Kim tell him she was on her way home and hoped to see him tonight.

Kim hung up and was ready to go, and they made their way out and said their good-byes.

Joy made her way home and walked straight upstairs to take a seat on her bed, deep in thought. She reached over and picked up the el she had sitting in the ashtray. Minke was her only thought as she allowed her mind to flow when she heard her phone vibrate.

She retrieved it from her purse thinking and hoping it was Minke, but to her surprise, it was Omari. She ignored it because she knew if he talked right he would end up in her bed. Only thing was, she knew Minke had a key to her house, and she really didn't want to give her love to another. So it wouldn't be good for Omari to come around while she was feeling like this.

Her phone began to vibrate again. She ignored the call but picked it up to call Sizemo. Why? She didn't really know.

He picked up on the first ring. "What the hell you want?" he answered, hyped up.

"Hi to you, fat boy. Don't get new," she said with a smile in her voice.

"What's going on with you this time of night? And, no, I ain't coming around there. You belong to my man." Sizemo laughed.

"Nigga, please, you crazier than a bitch, but know what, Sizemo? I'm getting tired of this shit. This nigga came back to me on that good shit, making me feel like I was that bitch and he was sorry for all the shit he did to me. But now I know that nigga doing his own thing and got me sitting here fucked up. I'm hurting inside, Sizemo, and I'm so lonely, I don't know what to do, ready to give a nothing-ass nigga some pussy. I've tried to play fair, but it's hard, real hard. I need love and attention too. I'm just talking to you because I have no one else to talk to."

Sizemo could hear the hurt in her voice.

Over the last several months Sizemo had seen Minke come in and express his love and concern to Alecia then string her along. They'd had conversation in confidence about her and other bitches he'd been fucking around with. He also knew about all the shit Minke had in his head about her, and that he had moved in with another girl because he didn't feel like he could trust Alecia like he used to, but wasn't ready to let her go.

He also knew about the Dominican thing in New York that had Minke open, and that she was one reason why he spent so much time out of town. Minke had explained that he loved Alecia like no other woman, but he didn't ever think he could look at her the same as when he was married to her. Minke actually had more of his heart and trust into his Dominican thing, which actually started off as a jump-off.

And the new thing in VA that he moved in with was a must. He had to have somebody, and somewhere in VA, that would make him feel comfortable, and it wasn't Alecia. She was mad cool, but she had become more like a friend.

Sizemo always understood that dudes play, but as the years passed, he had become close to girls. So close, he felt bad for playing them, because he knew they deserved better. So he came honest before someone got hurt.

His relationship with Alecia had been so cool, he actually cared about her. He really didn't care for the way Minke treated her. Not that he played her, but he played her openly, shitted on her like she was nothing, and talked to her any kind of way, always making her feel like she was beneath him, like it was a blessing to fuck with him. Something he'd heard Minke say on many occasions. But in this case, he was doing it to someone he'd been knowing for a long time, someone he cared about and had built a personal friendship with separate from theirs.

"Look, Alecia, we been friends a long time. Now me and Minke like brothers, and I can't go against my man, nor can I play him. I'm talking to you as if you were my sister. Open your eyes and look at my dude as a man. A man. Don't look at him as your kids' father, not as your husband, but as a man. Then make your decisions. I'm tired of you crying and being hurt and running around here fucked up all the time. My dude is in New York. When he come back, y'all need to sit down and come to some solid ground. When we talk, he talks about his disappointment with you and all your friends, and you talk the same shit on him."

"I ain't doing shit. I love that nigga like that, Sizemo. Anybody can see that shit."

"Yo, Joy, you must've forgot who you talkin to. This is me. My man have called me from your house at twelve, one in the morning while sitting in your house smoking an el, calling you, and you don't answer your phone. He told me about dude popping up at your house and how he had to get down or the nigga would of fucked you and him up in front of Juan and Q. Shit could have gotten real ugly, and his ass could've gotten locked up. When niggas start pulling burners and shit, it aint good. He could've caught a body. You know how he live and how we get down.

Look, I ain't taking sides, and you know this, but I'm sayin, don't talk to me like you ain't doing shit, because you doing you. But y'all need to sit the fuck down because the only way it's gonna work is if y'all come real with each other," he said, pulling up to Kim's condo.

"Yo, I just pulled up to your girl shit and getting ready to go in here and get nasty, straight freaky, then carry my ass home to my girl."

"That's nasty. I don't know why niggas do the shit y'all do."

"Yo, can't explain it to you, but that's how we do. All but Minke. He's true. He don't live like that. Never playing, that's my man," he said, laughing.

"Yeah, nigga, laugh at your own jokes. Handle your business. I'll holla tomorrow."

"Naw, I'm gonna check on you when I leave here on my way home. Don't answer the muthafuckin' phone and see what happen. I'm coming over there, and it won't be pretty," he said as if he was serious.

"Bye, fool," she said, hanging up.

Through all that conversation, at least he'd told her what she really wanted to know. Her man was in New York probably doing the same thing Sizemo was doing here.

As she thought about it, she caught a sad feeling. Then she realized that Sizemo had said he was going home to his girl each and every night, no matter what. She wasn't even that woman that Minke considered his main thing, the one he came home to every night. She really meant nothing to him.

She smiled, smirked, and shook her head to keep from crying. It was funny to her that her peoples had started calling her Pain as a joke, instead of Joy, because her attitude had become so hard and rude because of the pain she carried within her, making her unbearable sometimes. Her kids never knew who was gonna be coming home. All they knew was to stay out her living room and out her face, which wasn't hard, since they had their own rooms now. And work was the same.

The only exception was Minke. She was never rude with him. He dominated her, gave her a feeling of love and security, then he lost it. And after all these years, she was still chasing that feeling. That high of being Minke's girl, the woman he loved, wanted, desired, respected, and wanted to call wifey. But these days the chase was getting hard.

She stood up and took off her clothes, reached in her drawer that held all her toys and videos. Since Minke had found all her shit, it wasn't a secret anymore. And since he was hardly ever there, she thought, *Fuck it!* She grabbed her silver bullet and the white 10-inch dildo with the thick vein running up the side, which made it even wider. She'd nicknamed it Minke because pushing it up in her only brought him to mind.

She lay back and rubbed her already moist box, allowing her palm and fingers to gently slide across her clit, each time opening her legs wider because of the enticing feeling that came over her body each time. She reached for Minke and pushed him slowly inside her then turned him on low. Then she took her silver bullet and placed it on her clit, pulling juices already running onto her bullet, moving it slowly around on low. She let out a deep sigh of relief as her body began to soak in the feeling of ecstasy.

Just then her phone began vibrating.

"Damn!" she said out loud, reaching for the phone. "What, Omari?" she said, frustrated, before answering the phone. Then the picture of him eating her pussy flashed before her eyes, and the way he fucked would have her cumming all night, as horny as she was.

"Hello" she answered in a groggy voice as if he'd waken her out of her sleep.

"What up, Joy? I didn't think you were gonna answer," he said as if he was excited.

"What up, Omari? What you want?" she asked sleep-
ily.

"You. You still upset with me?"

"No, I'm over all that. I still think about you because
of all we been through. I can't just say, 'Fuck you.'" You
in my heart, but you did me wrong. Then you turned
around and disrespected me and put your hands on
me," she said sadly, and not really giving a damn. That
shit was over and done with.

"Joy, I am sorry. For real, baby, I am sorry. All that
shit wa'n't me. I was just messed up inside. You said
fuck me when I was depending on you, really depending on you."

"But I needed help. I was barely making it when you
took my car. You weren't helping me, and you tried to
hurt me worse."

"Well, I need you to forgive me. I miss you, and I really miss your love. I need you, baby," he said, almost
in tears.

"I need you too, Omari, and I miss you like crazy,
but . . ."

"But you with dude now, huh? That's your man, Joy?"
he asked sadly. "That's why you moved on me and didn't
let me know where you were? You didn't want me to
know where you lived?"

"No, after all that shit happened that night, he said
he wanted me to move for the safety of his kids, and he
said me too, but I know it was for his kids."

"So why you haven't contacted me? Why have you
ignored my calls? He be there with ya?"

"Omari, after that night when that shit happened,
he got us out of there. He told me not to have no more
dealings with you. He paid for me to move into my new
town house, he put up my deposit and paid my first and
second month's rent. That took almost three stacks.

Then he made me promise not to call or talk with you, and he would buy me a new car and take care of my rent."

"Damn! Seem like you better off without me."

"And you scared my kids. So they'll tell him if you come around. You know how Q talk."

"Yeah, but if you want to see me, you'll make a way. Shit! I got to understand if dude doing it like that. If he coming off like that, I can't compete. And I don't blame you for not doing nothing to fuck that up."

"And I won't. I would be crazy."

"Where he at now? I know he ain't there."

"He out of town. He don't stay here all the time even when he here, but he got a key and he may pop up. He a real street nigga. Do I have to explain all that?"

"No, I understand."

Omari wanted to believe what she was saying, but he didn't want to believe that she didn't want him. He figured she was staying away strictly because Minke was paying all her shit at the crib. If it wasn't true, that's what she put in his head, so he was rolling with it.

"So you don't miss me, Joy? You done wit' me?"

"Yes, I miss you, Omari. How can I forget what we had and how you been there for me? But you put my back against the wall."

"I need to see you. I miss you, baby. I miss the way you taste. I miss the way you feel. Come on, Joy, what's up? Stop denying me."

"I can't, Omari. If you get a room or something, I could meet you, but I can't mess up. I'm finally getting ahead." Joy needed him to understand this was gonna be on her terms.

"Girl, you know I ain't got no money. My shit ain't changed yet."

"So what, Omari? What am I to do?" she asked. *Show me, nigga, you understand the conditions.*

"So what? Let me come get in your bed," he said directly. "Fuck all this, man!"

"If I tell you where I live, Omari, you can't mess me up, for real. You got to call me first, and if I don't answer, leave it alone. You understand?"

"Okay, I got you. Now open the door," he said with a smirk.

"You at my door?" she asked, jumping up and throwing her toys back in the drawer. "I know you ain't. I don't know if my son 'sleep or not. And how—"

She heard a slight knock then "Open the door now."

She threw on her oversized green pajama silk top and fastened two buttons nervously as she made her way down the stairs to open the door. There stood that nigga that she really missed. The man she was so comfortable with that had really shown her love.

She let him in and locked the door then pulled him upstairs to her room and locked that door too.

Omari pulled her into his arms and squeezed her tight. "Joy, I've missed you, baby. Really, really missed you."

"I've missed you, baby, your touch, everything you use to do," she said, ready for him to eat her. She craved him, she was ready to beg for him, but she never got the chance.

He pushed her back on the king-sized bed Minke had gotten her, lifted her legs, and placed his tongue inside her already wet vagina. His lips resting on her lips, he licked and sucked her juices, enjoying the taste he'd been without for months.

She held in her yells and laid back shaking her head from side to side, her lips tightly pressed together, holding in her love sounds, as he worked his tongue in and out, up and down, from her asshole to her clit.

He took his hands and made her pussy lips wide, so he could get good suction on her clit, and flicked his tongue across it.

She placed her hands on his head lightly and opened her legs as wide as she could and concentrated on not losing her mind. "Come here, baby, please."

Omari stopped and quickly kicked off his shoes. Then he snatched off his clothes and climbed on the bed, and got on top of her in a sixty-nine position. He raised his right leg, allowing her to get full access to him, and she began sucking him like he had the last dick on earth. Joy licked and sucked until they fell into heaven.

Then he got up, turned around, and threw himself inside her, while staring into her face. "Open your eyes," he said.

And she did.

"I want you to know you ain't just fuckin'. You makin' love to yo nigga. Recognize me, baby," he said as he made love to her slowly.

Omari pulled out, and before she knew it, he was eating her again.

Then he was back inside her, throwing dick.

Then he was eating her again.

Before she came, he lifted himself up, keeping her lips wide and her clit exposed as he positioned himself to slide inside her and lay on her clit, and instead of pumping, he grinded while his satisfier only moved slightly.

Joy wrapped her legs around him as they bucked like animals and made animal sounds. She felt her body begin to cum.

The sounds she made in his ear took Omari over the edge, and his body tightened. He reached around her body, allowing his body to fold into her, and squeezed her as he bucked quickly inside her.

Joy heard a grunt and moan that let her know that he truly missed, and enjoyed her.

They lay exhausted, sweat gleaming from their bodies, and juices running between their legs. Omari lifted himself and rolled on his back, and she jumped up and went in the bathroom to clean up.

She returned with a warm washcloth and wiped him from the tip of his dick to the back of his balls. Then she licked him from the tip to back until he was hard again, and he had her bent over, legs spread, pounding her like no tomorrow.

Joy gave it back, allowing him to get up in her as deep as possible, where he would hit and make her pusssy make the gushing sounds.

Omari could really feel her squeezing on his dick, but when he reached around and palmed her breasts, which filled each hand, and massaged them, he got the extra stiffness he longed for, which excited her and gave her that sensation to keep her going.

His body felt so good, and he was about to cum, but he wanted her to cum with him, so he let her right breast go and reached down and fingered her clit, sending her bucking out of control as her juices flowed on his fingers.

Omari leaned back and spread her ass cheeks and slowly slid his middle finger in her ass. And she slowed down, allowing it to ease all the way in, until he could feel his finger riding on top of his dick, with only the thin layer of ridged skin separating his dick and finger. He then fucked with precision, straight in and out, wiggling his finger inside her ass.

Joy's breathing increased, her head dropped, and her mouth parted, and she concentrated on the greatest feeling she knew.

When she let out a moan, he felt a warm gush on his satisfier that he'd never felt before, and it sent him over the top, making him cum so hard. He then jammed himself inside of her with such force, his finger popped out her ass, and she fell flat as his body collapsed on top of hers. Omari was jerking uncontrollably, like he was having a seizure.

Joy turned to the side, and he slid behind her, never pulling out. And he wrapped her in his arms, and in silence they fell asleep.

The following morning Omari jumped up at the sounds of Joy's kids at her bedroom door.

"I'm coming down!" she yelled.

"I need to go?" Omari asked.

"Not unless you have somewhere to be. I'm not going in until one today. Be right back." She smiled. "Relax."

Joy went downstairs, took care of her kids, and got them out the door. She then made her way back upstairs. In seconds, she was laying in the middle of her bed, legs open, and Omari was slamming his dick inside of her slowly, staring down at her, and she was staring back, enjoying his every stroke.

While she held him in her arms, her eyes watered, and tears slowly ran down her face. That was when she realized she loved Omari, but she couldn't allow herself to fall for a broke-ass man. Not totally. She also loved Minke, but she was getting used to him not being there.

She wasn't used to Omari not being there, because he was the only man who needed her to survive, for his well-being, and she liked him being there. Omari gave his time, but not by choice, because he didn't have shit else to do. He wasn't a paper chaser like Minke and Sizemo. He was . . .

Joy didn't know what to think. All she knew was, she was happy this morning. Happier than she'd been in a long time.

"That was all that. Damn! I miss my girl."

"And I miss you, Omari. You just don't know how many times I wanted to call you, or answer your call. I'm doing what I have to do, not what I want to do. That's what it came to, for my kids and for myself," she said softly.

"Okay, I'm not gonna get in your way. I been known where you stay. At first, I was gonna kill your man, but I didn't want to kill your kids' father. So this is how I played it. I rode by many times and seen Juan hanging out several times. I love you, Joy. Nothing gonna keep you from me, so play your hand, but don't play me."

"I won't," she said, kissing him.

Right or wrong, Joy hadn't felt this good in a long time. Her life was balancing, and she wasn't feeling so messed up inside. She finally realized, as long as she had someone loving her, showing her attention, and placing her in the wifey position, it did wonders for her feelings of self-worth.

She cooked him breakfast, they sat and ate, talked, then showered together, before making her way out the door.

"So am I gonna see you later?" he asked slowly, shutting the door to her car.

"I want to. I'll call you and let you know."

"Let me know, Joy. I'm missing you already. Don't forget, up to several months ago, you came home every day to me and the kids. You don't miss that?" he asked, gleaming.

"I do, I really do," she answered, looking at him.

Standing there by her door, Omari had no idea how bad she wanted him there like that. If Minke wasn't gonna be there, by his own choice, then fuck him. No matter what he did for her financially and sexually, she was lonely, and she wanted her family.

"We'll talk later. I'll call you. Let me get over here," she said.

"Give me some change, man." Omari patted his pockets. "Shit! I'm cracked."

"Omari, I don't got no money," she said with a look that he knew so well.

"Kill that shit, Joy. You got a nigga taking care of you, paying all yo' shit, and you get to fuck up that phat-ass Verizon check. Please, give me some money."

"You went from change to some money." She looked in her purse.

"Man, give me some money. Look at the kicks, same jeans you seen me in when you had me scrambling out your house."

They both laughed.

"Shut up, boy," she said, still laughing. She knew he was still fucked up, but he was her boy, and had been there through some rough times.

"I know you ain't carrying around in your purse what I want." He smirked. "I'll follow you to the bank."

Joy shook her head and put the sixty dollars she had in her hand back in her purse.

She pulled up at work thinking about what Omari said when she gave him that three hundred dollars. She had asked him, "How you know where I live?"

"You put me down as an authorized user on your phone. So I called Cox and gave them the last four of your social, and they gave me your address, bill amount due, everything," he'd said, never cracking a smile.

CHAPTER 13

That muthafucka crazy, she thought, getting out of her car. She had a serious look on her face as she approached the building.

When the door swung open, she stepped back and gazed into the eyes of the most handsome man she'd laid eyes on in a long time. He was like no guy she'd been with. He was mature, and his wide, jet-black beard was trimmed perfectly, laying on his dark brown skin. Her eyes gazed on his full lips, and bright eyes with long eyelashes.

He smiled, and she exhaled.

"You okay, baby?" he asked in a voice that actually soothed her.

"Yes, just beautiful. I don't wanna box you," she said with a smirk, throwing her hands up.

"No, we don't want that," he replied, looking into her cute, young-looking face that revealed some age, from the darkness around her eyes.

He took in her smooth, flawless caramel skin. Then his eyes glanced down to her large breasts that couldn't be hidden behind those arms. He looked down at the short, little, fat girl and was amazed at how beautiful she was.

"My name is Andre Brooks." He smiled, showing his shining white teeth.

"You said that like you're important." She smirked.

"I am, baby. You better Google that shit."

"Alecia," she said, sticking her hand out.

"Nice to meet you. What do you like to do?"

Andre's question caught her off guard, but she bounced back quickly. "Bowling, Jillian's, walk the beach, whatever. Long as I ain't bored."

"I'll take you bowling, to Jillian's, the beach, if you go to a party with me on Saturday."

"Where? Is it a dressy occasion?"

"Semi-formal. So, what time am I picking you up tonight?"

"What time am I meeting you?"

"No. What time am I picking you up, like the lady you are, for our date this evening?" he asked with no smile, showing his seriousness while staring her down.

"Six thirty. I got to work. Can't stay out late."

"I'll call you when I'm on my way and get the address."

Andre handed her his BlackBerry Curve, and she put in her number and handed it back to him. Then he pressed send, and her phone rang.

"Lock me in, so you'll know who's calling and always pick up."

Alecia walked into the building as he held the door.

Andre walked away knowing he was a winner. He'd always liked thick girls and pretty girls, and now he had the best of both worlds.

Joy walked in her house and went straight to the shower. It was the first time in a minute that someone was taking her on a real date, and she wanted to know for sure he was really coming. Dudes these days were coming at her all kinds of ways, but she didn't care. This evening, whether he showed up or not, once she was dressed, she was going somewhere.

When 6:15 rolled around, she began to worry. She was starting to think he had stood her up. But then her phone rang. It was Andre. She gave him directions, and he was there fifteen minutes later. Next time he called, he was out front.

She came out wearing her short, fitting, army-green knit skirt with a beige button-down top that came down past her waist, camouflaging her stomach, with the four-inch heels, which made her seem taller. And every step made the big, beautiful, black woman look so graceful and so stunning.

As she gave the handsome man sitting in the new platinum Buick LaCrosse a wide smile, he jumped out the car and opened her door.

"Thank you." She respected Andre for being a gentleman.

"You look stunning, darling," he said, looking at her and her beautiful smile.

"So what's the plan?"

"Well, we going to Granby Street Lounge downtown where one of my boys playing tonight," he said, pulling off.

"He's in a band?"

"Yes, he plays the bass."

"Thought we were going bowling?"

Andre smiled. "I don't think that was your plan, not dressed like that. It's either the lounge, restaurant, or a movie."

Alecia didn't respond. Dressed in the fly shit, she wanted to make an impression, not knowing she already did.

They arrived at The Time, and the band had already set up. Andre's friend came and greeted him, and showed him the table he had reserved. They sat down, and a bottle of wine was brought to the table.

Andre took the initiative and poured their glasses. She didn't care for wine, but she never said anything or showed it. She sipped and sat like a lady as the five-man band played easy-listening jazz that had her body and head moving slowly and falling into a trance, making for a romantic evening.

Andre talked softly, his arm resting on the back of her chair, and as the wine disappeared and the music played, she slid closer, until she almost rested in his arms.

The evening was beautiful. When they pulled back up at her house, there was about thirty young'uns hanging on East Hastings. Amongst the crowd was her son Juan.

"You don't have to walk me to the door," she said.

Andre ignored her. He got out the car and opened her door, stuck his hand out and helped her out the car, then walked her up to her door.

"You left here happy and with a smile, and I returned you the same way, I hope, a little happier and with a better feeling."

"A great feeling. You made me feel like a lady. And I would like to thank you for a beautiful evening," she said with a smile. "Can I ask you something?" she asked.

"Yes, anything."

"Do you have kids?"

"Yes, three."

"Are you married? These are questions I had all night, but it was never the right time."

"I did that on purpose, Alecia," he said, looking at her. "I wanted the evening to be relaxing. Two people who just met enjoying each other's company without stress, just out for a nice time, with no wonders or attitudes. And it worked for the most part. No, I'm not married."

"And how old are you?"

"Forty," he said proudly. "And you?"

"Thirty-three," she said. "Damn! You look good. I was thinking thirty-five at the most."

"Thank you. I was giving you thirty, but it didn't matter. I been feeling you since I almost knocked you out." He laughed.

"You not a married woman with kids, are you?"

"No, I'm a divorced woman with two kids," she said smiling. "That's my son over there with his pants hanging off his ass."

"Which one?" he asked as they shared a laugh.

"I enjoyed your company tonight, Alecia."

"And I really enjoyed yours, Andre. I'm impressed."

"So tomorrow six thirty, bowling attire."

"No doubt. See you at six thirty. Guess you'll be calling when you pull up."

Andre leaned in, hugged her, and kissed her cheek. "Tomorrow," he said, allowing his warm breath to hit her cheek.

Alecia got another whiff of his Curve cologne that had her not minding at all when he eased close to her in the lounge, to support her body.

She walked inside feeling like she was on cloud nine. So turned-on, she went upstairs and pulled out her short, sexy, black nightie with the spaghetti straps. She stripped naked and allowed the piece of silk to slide down on her body, climbed in her bed with phone in hand, and returned Minke's call.

He had a lot to say, questioning her about not answering her phone, verbally abusing her as always, and making threats. Usually it would hurt her to tears. And tonight it hurt her as always, but she couldn't cry. When Minke slammed the phone down, she thought about the days that he loved and respected her. Now she didn't know what he wanted.

She lay back, hurt at the words that came out of Minke's mouth, and frustrated because she'd allowed it. She shook her head, staring at her phone, and dialed Omari.

CHAPTER 14

"Yes, Andre, yes," Alecia whispered in his ear as he slowly slid inside her.

He'd been eating her for the last half hour, and she came after fifteen minutes. But he never stopped, even after she tried to push his head away.

Andre gripped her legs and buried his face in her womanhood and slurped up every drop of cum she had to give. And now he was trying to fit his huge dick inside of her with no condom.

She took deep breaths with every inch that eased inside of her. When he was in as far as any man had been, she exhaled, only to inhale as more dick kept coming. Not to mention, he was so thick, her walls were being stretched, sending sensations of pleasure through her body. She opened her mouth, trying to breathe, slowly shaking her head, not believing he had a real magic stick. Once he was finally in, he began to throw it like he was a real fucksman.

Alecia spread her legs wide as possible, trying to receive all the pleasure he had to give as he pounded harder. The pain turned to pleasure, and then he let out a loud grunt. His eyes closed, and his mouth fell open as his body began to shake, and drool dripped from his mouth onto her chest. He stayed in his push-up position and slid back slowly, pulling his dick out of her.

As she slowly caught her breath, she watched him walk into the bathroom and get a rag to wipe himself. She stared at his 11-inch dick that was so thick, it was surreal. She wanted him back inside of her. He brought her a rag, and she wiped off. Then he climbed in and wrapped his arms around her, making her feel loved and appreciated.

"You okay, baby?" She was hoping he was like Omari, Minke, or Booby, who had to get at least two nuts before even thinking about stopping.

"Yes. Wonderful, Alecia. I'm truly feeling you." He smiled. "I couldn't feel better. And are you okay?"

"Yes, you're the perfect man," she blurted out. *But, yo' ass need to finish*, she thought.

They had come back to his house after the party, feeling nice. Soon as they were in the door, he was on her. She didn't usually kiss dudes, but he was so fine and had been so sweet, she decided to give him whatever he wanted. So when he threw his tongue in her mouth, she opened it, and they went at it. To her surprise, it felt good.

They relaxed on his brown leather loveseat, as his hands reached down and untied the black wrap dress, allowing it to fall open, exposing the black panties and bra. He reached behind her and undid her bra, lifting it and watching her huge, pretty breasts drop. He took hold of them with both hands like a young boy overjoyed with two new toys.

As he sucked and licked her nipples, she stared at him, not feeling a thing. But knowing every man's desire was to put them in their mouth and suck, she let him. It would be fifteen minutes before he would come up for air. She relaxed, not moved at all, until he reached between her legs and threw his middle finger inside her then his index finger and dug roughly. Then her juices began to flow.

Andre jumped up and pulled her to his room, laying her down, pulling off her panties, and burying his head into her musty pussy.

They had danced all night, and she knew she would've usually wiped herself fresh. But he took charge, and if he didn't mind, then who was she to say anything.

She opened her legs and allowed him to do his job, while she rubbed his head and enjoyed him. She felt herself about to cum, hoping he would stop and make love to her, but he didn't. He allowed her to cum until she was drained.

She was done, not wanting to be touched, but he tightened his grip and continued. This, she didn't like, but after a few minutes, it was feeling good again.

Her body began to react when he removed his clothes and climbed on top of her. For two minutes, he made her feel, and gave her, something she'd never felt, and then filled her with cum.

As she lay with his arms wrapped around her and his hand resting on her breast, she was wide awake, but he was sleeping. She was hoping that big snake resting in her ass-crack would rise up and ease up in her, but it didn't happen.

That's when she realized, because a man knows how to eat pussy and got a big dick, that don't make him a good lover. But the way he had taken her out to the lounge one night, bowling the next, Jillian's the day after that, walks along the Chesapeake Bay, and dinner every night, that kept her wanting him more and more.

On top of that, he respected her and treated her like a woman that he wanted in his life, and as long as he kept coming like that, she was gonna be there like his woman, giving him whatever he wanted.

The next morning she woke to his snake trying to rise between her legs. She smiled and lifted her leg, giving him an open invitation, and he slowly eased in. Once he was enveloped in her sweetness, she put her leg down and stuck her ass out and looked at the clock beside his bed. It was 7:59. She closed her eyes and enjoyed her body being slammed in and out of, as delight took over. Then she heard him moan.

Andre lay still as she kept pushing back, trying to reach her orgasm, but it was no use. He was soft, and with her wetness and all the cum he put inside of her, it slid out. Frustrated, she looked at the clock again—8:01.

When he got up and went to the bathroom, she grabbed her phone. Eight missed calls, one from Kim, two from Omari, and five from Minke.

Damn! she thought. She was gonna have to go through with this nigga. She got up and went to the bathroom to clean up. "I got to go to church this morning. I need to get ready to go, okay," she told him.

"No problem, baby," he said, getting out her way and throwing on something.

CHAPTER 15

All the way home she prayed nobody was outside her house, and her prayers were answered. She walked inside, and before she could call anybody, her phone rang. It was Minke.

She went and lay down and answered as if she was waking up. "Hello," she said groggily.

"Where the fuck you were last night, Alecia?" Minke yelled.

"Went out for some drinks," she said, still acting as if she was 'sleep.

"Yeah, right! You on some bullshit. What time you get home?" he demanded to know.

She saw he had called between one and 2:30. "About three. Kim dropped me about three something," she said, in case he'd come by.

"I needed you last night, and you left me hanging," he said, playing on her emotions. He knew she was lying because he was at her house 'til six. Then he had to ride to D.C. with one of his boys on some money shit.

"I'm fucked up in D.C. I needed you last night, and you were nowhere. Yo, I need you to come get me. I'll give you five hundred. Come get me," he said seriously.

He wanted her to come to D.C., and he was going to confront her again. And if she lied, he was gonna leave her ass in D.C. for the peoples to find her.

"Okay," she said, wanting money, and forgetting she was supposed to be faking sleep.

He caught it and told her to come on, and she put on her slippers and left out, headed to D.C.

When she got there, he guided her to the hotel in Northwest Washington. He felt like he wanted to fuck her once more before he strangled her ass, so he acted real sweet, as if he was thankful she'd come. He went downstairs and got some roses.

When she arrived, he had roses on the floor and bed. She smiled on the outside, while feeling real funny inside.

Minke hugged her tight. Knowing she couldn't tell him no, he lied, saying how much he missed and wanted her, as he opened the same dress Andre did, and took off the same bra and panties, laid her back, and threw his dick in her.

Alecia looked at the clock as he began pumping in and out of her. It was 1:45. She closed her eyes and allowed him to finish what Andre couldn't. She came two times in the twenty minutes Minke made love to her.

Then he jumped up and walked in the bathroom to wipe himself off and came back and wiped her. Before she could close her legs, he was back inside her, pumping again.

Before, he could see the expression on her face that told him she enjoyed him making love, but this time, minutes before he came, he could see her dying out. He wasn't inside her two minutes, and he could see her pressing her lips together and twitching because she was done, so he pumped harder.

Five minutes later, he could see the agony he was causing her. Her pussy was getting dry, and he was still forcing it, causing the look of pain to spread all across her face. So he fucked harder, to make himself cum, which lasted more than five minutes.

She was so happy when he came, she put down her legs and sighed relief.

Minke smiled inside. He knew she had fucked some-body else and was lying to him. He wanted her to feel his pain. This was her punishment. He collapsed be-hind her, just like Andre did, and held her in his arms.

"God! That was wonderful. I love you," he said, not lying, though he hated her at that point in time.

"I love you too, Minke," she responded, not lying, but not wanting what he was offering at that time, except for that five hundred dollars.

He held her tight as if he didn't ever want to let her go. While his dick rested in the crack of her ass, and he was waiting to get hard again, he was thinking about some of the nastiest shit he could, to show her that she can't fuck two.

Alecia lay there in pain from him banging her pussy till it was dry. It felt sore and irritated. She prayed he wouldn't get hard again.

When she felt his dick stiffening between her legs, she tried to get up, but he pulled her close, pushed her over on her stomach, and slid back in, pumping like a mad man.

He felt her squirming to get away, but he wouldn't let up.

"It's hurting, Minke. I don't want to do it no more."

"Girl, I'm about to cum. Give me a sec, baby. I been missing you. You got me like this." He flipped her over, so he could see the discomfort and agony on her face. It worked. The more hurt he saw, the harder he got.

Five minutes later, when the cum he'd let out dried up, he looked down at her and could clearly see the tor-ture he was putting her through. And as a tear dropped from the corner of her eye, he grabbed her legs, threw them up almost behind her head, pressing her stomach into her breasts, knowing it was hard for her to breathe or move.

As she lay balled up, her privates wide open, he whispered in her ear, "I love you," and continued to pound away, until he felt the wetness from the tears hit his face.

Minke smiled, feeling good about all the physical abuse he was afflicting on her. He grunted and jammed his dick hard as he could into her, and the high-pitched screech and flow of tears did it. He began to cum so hard, his body jerked, and he collapsed.

Alecia turned over on her stomach and lay there motionless.

He looked over at her, knowing she wasn't shit, but she still got to him. He couldn't kill her, but he wanted to, so all he could do was bring her any type of pain to her life that he could.

He got up and went to the bathroom, where she walked in to him wiping off. He saw her and started scrubbing more intensely.

"It wouldn't be me if I wa'n't honest."

"What, Minke?" she said sadly.

"I'm scrubbing like this, because yo pussy ain't never smell like this. Bitch, yo pussy stank, like you been fuckin'. Like you climbed out a nigga bed and came straight to me. Damn, Lecia! You need to check yo'self," he said, walking out.

Alecia closed the door and sat on the toilet and cried silently. She didn't want him to know he got to her like that, but he made her feel lower than low.

Minke sat on the bed smoking, knowing he'd got her ass. He knew she was in the bathroom fucked up. *Maybe she'll change her damn ways,* he thought. *Trifling bitch!*

***

They made it back to Norfolk about eight o'clock.

Minke chilled out at the house for about an hour. Then he had Sizemo pick him up. He told her he had money to collect and would see her later on with the five hundred.

It wasn't 'till the first of the month he gave her five hundred dollars then told her he was short and could only give her three hundred on the eight-hundred-dollar rent that was due.

She was mad as hell and just wanted him to stay away from her. She was determined to get over him. He wasn't gonna do this to her again.

Over the next couple months, Minke made himself scarce. At first she loved that she could move without worrying about him popping up and causing confusion in her world.

She was seeing Andre on the regular, and their time was spent mostly at his house, but every time she stayed over, she would wake up with so many missed calls and messages, it was scary.

By this time, Omari had damn near become a stalker. She would come home, and he would be sitting in front of her house like a lost puppy.

Then one morning she realized he was really a problem when he started explaining to her how much he loved her, that he didn't want to live without her. He actually started crying and begging her to stop playing him, saying he'd rather die than be without her. She tried to explain to him that he was being silly and to stop acting so crazy, but he fell in her arms and cried.

Joy felt so bad for him, but Andre had come in and made such an impact on her, nothing and nobody was going to come before him.

She hugged Omari and kept telling him that Andre was just a friend that she used for money, that he was nice but not her type. She assured him that he was too old and corny for her, and she wouldn't dream of sleeping with him, but if he wanted to give his money away, then she had to take it.

Then she gave Omari some good sex, and all his insecurities eased up, and he went away happy as a child on a playground. He'd turned soft. He'd turned into a dude she'd lost respect for, and she was slowly trying to show him that she wasn't for dealing with him like that.

He'd catch her home every now, and she'd ignore his calls most of the time. And when he did catch her, she would allow him every now and then to taste her love, if she was in the mood. Other than that, she was losing interest and didn't want his friendship to go anywhere.

CHAPTER 16

One night Alecia dropped by Andre's house after work. He had flowers on his doorstep, that led through his house, up to his bedroom, into his bathroom, where rose petals floated on top of the bubbles. He told her to undress and to get into the Jacuzzi tub.

As she sat in the hot water, her body relaxed. He got the gauze sponge and squirted some Warm Vanilla Sugar body wash on it and slowly began to bathe her. Her mind floated away as the sounds of Joe eased out of the Bose radio in the room to the flickering candle lights bouncing off the mirrors and walls.

He slowly ran the sponge all over her body, and she leaned back when he reached down and rubbed between her legs and rested his lips on her breasts. Her eyes popped open as she felt the vibrating dildo slowly go inside of her. She closed them back and smiled when the stimulator rested on her clit, sending vibrations through her entire body.

He continued until her body began to shake. Then he kissed her deeply, and she hugged him and squeezed. "I'm falling for you, Alecia," he said softly into her ear.

"I *been* fell for you, sweetie. You are a godsend," she said staring at him, not believing a man could be this sweet and attentive.

He smiled at her remark. "Oh yeah, sent here for you, you and only you. I want you here with me, Alecia, every day and night. I don't ever want to be without you."

"Do you know what you asking, Andre? I'm a package, and my kids ain't no joke."

"I been thinking about it, and I need and want you."

"I'm really loving you, Andre, but I want to buy my own home. I been working towards it. I really got to have my own, unless I'm married. And I know you ain't ready for that," she said, looking at him.

"Naw, baby. I just got out of all that. Yes, I care, but that's not what I want right now."

So you want the milk but don't want to buy the cow, she thought to herself. But she also realized this man came in the door treating her like a queen and not asking for anything in return. All he'd given her, she wanted to give.

"But I'll tell you what. I'll help you with the intentions of being with you. If it don't work out, I'll just move out, back into one of my houses I rent out. We'll make it work. I can't ever lose you, baby. I've already fallen in love." Andre looked down at the disappearing bubbles.

She reached out and placed her hands on his chin and lifted his head, looked into those eyes that made her melt. "And I love you, Andre."

Their lips came together and opened, and their tongues began to explore.

He stood up and removed his wife-beater, exposing the tattoos that covered his body. Then he dropped his boxers.

That had her mouth watering. She licked her lips and thought of giving him head, but decided against it. She wanted to, but it wasn't the right time. She wasn't gonna put herself out there right now.

Andre climbed in the large garden tub, and she spread her legs, allowing her feet to rest on the outside. Then he leaned between her legs and entered her slowly and began to fill her body up. As he moved, her breathing increased, and she felt sensations going through her body, preparing for him to cum, but he didn't.

The warm water didn't let him get the full affect of her and he began to gyrate harder until sweat dripped from his body.

She screamed, "Yes, baby, yes," as she came again, sending him over the top as he exploded inside of her.

Andre struggled to keep his balance as his legs weakened, trying to get out the tub.

After Alecia washed herself again and got out, they dried off and laid across the bed, and he held her as they looked at *The First 48*.

Then when she realized the time, she made a move. She had to get home to her kids.

CHAPTER 17

When Alecia arrived at her house, she decided she wanted a hot shower before climbing in her bed. She allowed the steaming water to beam down on her, until she was startled by the curtain being pulled back.

"What up, baby?" Minke asked. "Damn! You sexy." He reached out and cupped one of her breasts in his hand and smacked her on her ass before walking out.

Damn! she thought, finishing up her shower.

When she came out, Minke was laying in the bed smoking. She lotioned herself up and reached in her drawer and pulled out her pajama pants and a T-shirt.

"When we start sleeping with clothes on?" Minke was holding his hard dick under the cover.

"I'm tired, Minke. I'm going to sleep," she said, putting on her pants and top.

"Shit, baby! You ain't seen me in a minute," he said with attitude. "Don't act like you ain't trying to get a nigga straight."

"You don't want none of this stankin' pussy. Ain't that what you said?" she replied climbing in bed.

He hugged her. "Go ahead with that shit."

She turned to him. "I don't know why you said that, but that hurt me. And it don't make me want to be with you. I'm going to sleep. Please don't mess with me."

He didn't take her seriously; she had never told him no.

He reached out and tried to pull her pants off.

She stopped him. "I'm serious. Do not fuck with me! I know you know what *no* means."

"Fuck you talkin' to?" he said, reachin out, trying to pull her pants down.

"Stop, Minke!" she said firmly, but not yelling because of the kids. She tried to get out of bed.

He jumped up and slammed her back down. Grabbing a pants leg in each hand, he snatched them off, almost pulling her off the bed.

When she tried to raise up, he got a fistful of hair and pulled her back down to the bed. Then he got on top of her and forced himself between her legs, guiding himself inside of her.

She fought, but was no match for him.

He pushed deep inside of her with every stroke, which didn't hurt because she was wet from Andre's cum still draining, and the water from the shower. But she cried until he was finished.

He got up and went in the bathroom and washed off.

"Fuck is wrong with you?" he asked, coming out.

"Nothing. I just don't want this shit no more."

"You got me fucked up. You belong to me. Don't get this shit twisted. You'll end up out this bitch by your gotdamn self trying to make it. What? You fuckin' with the next nigga? Huh?"

"Stop yellin', Minke." Alecia sighed.

"I pay for this shit. Don't tell me how to fuckin' talk. I'm a grown muthafuckin' man. Don't get fucked up, Alecia," he said, putting his finger to her head. "Let me get the fuck outta here before I fuck you up." He started throwing on his clothes.

Alecia lay in silence, tears streaming down her face.

"God, please. Please help me to get away from him. You know what I can bear, and I can't take no more!" she cried out loud.

***

While Joy was driving the following morning, she thought about Andre and what he'd done to bring her day to a perfect end, and the conversation they'd had about her buying a home and him being there.

The way he treated her made her feel like she was worth a million, the way he talked to her made her feel admirable, the way he made love to her made her feel delicate, and the way he looked at her through those appealing eyes of his fascinated her. In his eyes, she could see a compassionate, trusting, loving man that had in him all she could ever ask for, but she could clearly see all this crumbling down if he found out about Omari or Minke.

As soon as Minke crossed her mind, and what he pulled last night, and all the shit that came with him, her smile turned upside down. She envisioned his actions and how he made her feel. The way he treated her made her feel dreadful, the way he talked to her, looked at her, made her feel less than, and anytime he touched her, or called himself making love to her, she would feel disgusting.

Her phone rang as she listened to the *Steve Harvey Morning Show*. The number and name that showed up brought a feeling lower than she already felt. It was Minke.

Damn! I don't feel like going through this mess this morning. "Hello," she answered in a frustrated voice.

"Fuck is wrong with you?" he said angrily.

"Nigga, you is stressing the fuck out of me every time you come around. You need to chill the fuck out. I can't keep taking this shit." Joy said it so quick, she stunned herself. She had never come at him like that.

"Bitch! You better recognize. I ain't one of these country-ass VA niggas you been fuckin' with!" he shot back at her.

"Nigga, please leave me the fuck alone. I'm done with you. Don't call me no more." She hung up the phone.

He called back several times, and she ignored him.

Just when she was about to answer yelling, she looked at the phone, and it was Andre. She took a deep breath. "Hello." she answered in a calm, pleasing voice.

"How my lady doing this morning?"

His cool, pleasant voice made her smile and blush. "Your lady doing fine. Now that you called, I'm doing better than that," she said, stroking his ego.

Andre blushed. He was really feeling like she was his lady because she'd said it.

"And how are you this morning, baby?" she added, putting it on thick.

"Good. But it would have been much better if you were beside me this morning when I opened my eyes."

"Better for you, or better for him?" she asked, smiling.

"I would have been happy. He would have been happier than a muthafucka, hard as he was."

They shared a laugh.

She told him, "You laughin', but you serious as hell."

"Alecia, I'm headed to the gym. I just wanted to check on you and see if we were doing lunch today."

"Sure. Twelve thirty."

"See ya then. Keep smiling."

"Don't change on me," she said, seriously.

"This me, baby, this me." Andre hung up.

Joy couldn't wait for twelve thirty. She was feeling like a young girl on her first date. He excited her, brought back that feeling that she'd been missing for a long time.

***

When Andre pulled up at 12:30, Joy was already downstairs. She hopped in the black Magnum and leaned over and gave him a kiss.

He smiled. "How are you?"

"I'm doing fine, Andre," she said with a happy expression. "How are you? How was your workout?"

"I know you were talking about buying a house. I don't know how serious you were, but how soon were you trying to move on that? Were you really serious?"

"Yes, I was serious. Why? You gonna help me? You know something?"

"I been investing in real estate a minute," he said, matter-of-fact like. "I buy and flip houses all the time. I have a loan officer that do all my deals, I have a realtor that find my properties, and I have an attorney to close all my homes. So I can put you in, and they'll walk you through the entire process, if you ready."

"Where do I start? Help me. I'm not scared to ask for some help. I never did this before. Well, I've owned a house before, but it was my ex's," she said, letting him in. "I never bought one myself."

Andre picked up the phone and dialed his loan officer, and Joy was on the phone for ten minutes, giving him all her information, and answering a series of questions about her finances before she hung up.

She told Andre, "He said he'll call me back shortly."

As they sat in P.F. Chang's talking and enjoying their time, Joy's phone rang.

It was the loan officer letting her know that she had been pre-qualified for $170,000, and that he wanted to meet with her the following day so he could get the documents to support what she had told him, which could get her and her realtor a preapproved letter that would be good as cash.

She let him know that she didn't want her payments to be over $1,100 a month. He understood and told her that he would make the letter for $150,000, and she would not want to go over that.

They set up a time, and she got off the phone overjoyed.

Joy was asking Andre all kinds of questions all the way back to work. He gave her the number to his realtor and told her to give him a call.

Everything was in order, and the hunt was on. Joy was ready for this, and Andre could tell.

Ten and a half months had passed, and Joy's lease was about to expire. She was going to be giving her thirty-day notice in two weeks, and she already had a closing date on her new three-bedroom, two-and-a-half bath, two-story brick home with a loft and a garage.

The realtor had found her a bank-owned property that was only three years old. New, it sold for $187,000, but whoever bought it, couldn't afford it, so the bank took it back and put it back on the market for $150,000 so it could sell fast.

Her realtor told her to offer $140,000, so her payment would be right where she wanted it to be, and to even ask for all closing costs. They took it and agreed to pay all closing.

She was set to close in five weeks. In that time she was to take a class in Virginia Beach so she could receive a grant where the city would pay her down payment. All she would have to bring to the table were her pre-paid, estimated to be $1,100. She couldn't've been happier.

***

A couple of weeks later, Joy was sitting in her living room looking at *Law and Order, SVU* when her phone rang.

"I'm on the way around there. I was just making sure you was still going to Kim cousin party," Malaina said to Joy. Kim was throwing her cousin a bachelorette party, and they had planned to go.

Malaina pulled up twenty minutes later and came inside so they could smoke an el while Joy put on her finishing touches.

On her way out, Joy called Lady but got no answer. She figured she was in the shower, so she decided to go by her house and get her, since it was on the way.

As she was pulling in front of Lady's house, she saw a familiar car parked, and before she could say a word, Malaina yelled out, "Ain't that Minke car?"

"Hell, yeah! That his shit. I know that muthafucka ain't," Joy said, surprised.

"What the fuck is your man doing around this bitch house, Joy?"

"I don't know, but I know this nigga ain't fuckin' her!" Joy yelled. "I know that bitch ain't fuckin' Minke and smiling in my goddamn face! I know she ain't!"

Joy had Malaina dial Lady's phone, and Lady answered. Malaina talked while Joy dialed Minke phone, and heard it ring in the background. Lady told Malaina she would meet them at the party, she had some money to finish getting, she would be about an hour.

Joy hadn't talked to Minke in about a week. They weren't talking much since she cursed his ass out and told him not to call no more.

About forty-five minutes later, Minke hit Joy's phone, talking real sweet. She asked him where he was, and he told her he was on the Eastern Shore, headed for the bridge, coming back from New York, and he wanted to see her later.

She told him she would call him when she got back home and hung up.

Joy thought he had hurt her as much as he could, but her heart fell to her stomach again, like it had done so many times before.

"Damn, girl! What do I do?" Joy asked sadly. She'd had him on speaker, and when he lied, she and Malaina looked at each other.

Malaina could see the hurt in her girl's face and could hear it in her voice.

Joy pulled the car over, her eyes filled with tears.

"Come on, Joy, don't let him do this to you again. Don't do it, Joy."

Malaina reached out and hugged her girl, and Joy fell in her arms and let it go. She cried so hard, Malaina thought this was it. Her girl was going to have a breakdown.

"Fuck him, Joy! He not worth it. You see now, for real. He ain't shit, and he can't say shit to get out of this. You see it for yourself. A lot of shit can come at you, and people can tell you shit, but when you see with your own two eyes, it can't be denied." Malaina tried to comfort her friend, letting her know, it was what it was, and to get over it.

"I know, girl, I know. But it still hurt, Malaina. It hurt so bad." Joy wiped her face, trying to pull herself together. "I been done, girl, but I just can't believe this shit. And then that bitch hanging with us, smiling all in my face. Oh, no, she gettin' ready to see how this Brooklyn bitch get down."

"Calm down now. Don't do shit stupid over their triflin' ass. You got everything going your way these days. Don't fuck it up."

"Fuck that! I don't give a damn!" she yelled out of control. "I bet they pay for that shit. I hope he enjoyed that pussy, because it's gonna cost him his life. He think my sister Queen got Hitler. Bitch nigga, you ain't seen shit yet."

They arrived at the party and parked in the parking lot of the hotel downtown Norfolk. She had to roll a Dutch and sit in the parking lot and take it to the head, to calm herself down, before going inside.

CHAPTER 18

On the other side of town, Minke was kicked back in the chair that sat in the lounge area of Lady's oversized master bedroom, his Rocawear jeans pulled down, bunched on top of his new butter Timbs, receiving some of the best head he'd ever experienced in this lifetime. He knew he was wrong for even accepting her invitation the other week when he ran into her at Upscale nightclub.

That night Lady eased up to him and asked what he was drinking then returned fifteen minutes later with the double shot of Rémy. He thanked her and thought she would keep it moving, but she started conversation like she really knew him.

It was innocent until she asked why he never came her way to party with some of the girls, like the other ballers in the city did. He let her know that she did his girl head and that wa'n't no shit he got down with, he actually wanted to work things out with his kids' mother. Alecia was that real-ass bitch, they both were from BK, and she truly understood the shit in him that kept him going and knew how to handle him.

Lady was so offended, she sweetly burst his bubble, telling him about some of Joy's escapades. He responded by holding his cool, even though it fucked him up inside.

He still let her know that her team was still too close to home and he would pass.

When he thought she would walk away, Lady looked him in his face and told him that he must want to fuck with the queen, since the other bitches didn't have his interest. That left a confused look on Minke's face. But it was washed away when she slid her number in his hand and asked him if Joy controlled him and his dick, that she didn't take him as one of those niggas who let a bitch tell him what he could do with his dick, before she walked off.

Later that night when she was leaving, she came by him and hugged him good night and whispered in his ear that she was going home and would be waiting on his call. He kept telling himself that it wasn't gonna happen, until he left the club with those shots of Rémy dwelling inside him and ended up at Alecia house and she wasn't home.

After two calls and smoking a Dutch, he called Lady. On his way over, he told himself, if he had to work for it, or if she wanted him to spend money, it wasn't happening. But to his surprise when he walked inside her house, she invited him straight to her room.

He walked behind her, watching her ass sway side to side through the long emerald green nightgown. He sat down on her bed as she lit a Backwood and handed it to him. He leaned back and put the Backwood to his lips.

While he took in the good taste of exotic weed, she reached down and began to massage his manhood. As it hardened, she unzipped his pants, releasing his throbbing member, and before he knew it, she was on her knees, pleasuring him for minutes, before undressing him completely.

As Minke stood there naked, his dick in one hand and the el in the other, Lady lifted her nightgown and got on the bed on all fours with her legs wide, and ass up high, exposing her big, pretty, bald womanhood.

He reached in his pocket and threw on the Ultra Thin Trojan and slid inside of her. It felt so good, he didn't last as long as he usually would have. Once he came, he felt so guilty, he finished the el and made his exit, not caring if she ever gave him some pussy again.

But ever since Joy told him to fuck off, he'd been using Lady up, enjoying her every way possible. And every time she had some new shit with her. Always had on some sexy shit to make his dick harder and harder. And she drank and smoked, which made the evening flow. Even though he knew it wasn't right, he still couldn't stay away.

Tonight was no different.

When he came in this time, she wore a royal blue negligee that came down across her breast, barely covering her thick, erect nipples. They made it upstairs and sat in the lounge chair. Like always, she had an el already rolled.

As he lit it, she walked over to her CD player and turned it on, and the R. Kelly came flowing through. Lady began to dance and move so seductive, he instantly began to rise. When she threw her leg up on the side of the chair and he saw that the negligee came with a slit in it between the legs for easy access to her love, he was about to bust.

Lady stood him up and removed his Rocawear T-shirt and wife-beater. Then she began to kiss on his neck, sending shivers down his side, as she made her way down his developed chest.

Minke balled his fist and tensed up as she took his nipples into her mouth and licked and sucked. He thought he was gonna lose it, until she unbuckled his pants. And when they fell to the floor, she took his dick into her wet, warm mouth.

Minke's knees became weak. The sight of Lady on her knees, sucking his dick, holding his balls in her hand as she licked his shaft up and down, taking the head and slowly moving her tongue around it in a circular motion around the indented area that separated the head from the shaft, made it hard to keep his composure.

He knew she was about her business when she, all of a sudden, took his entire dick in her mouth and sucked him in. That had him shooting a hot load of semen down her throat. And she never stopped making sure he stayed hard.

Lady jumped on his dick instantly. He wasn't the hardest, but he wanted to fuck the hell out of her. But when that slick, warm, snug pussy wrapped around him, his dick stiffened up to full potential, and he threw it in her royally. Lady held on for dear life, both arms wrapped around his neck, until he exploded again.

Minke fell back in the chair, his body drained, and Lady fell into his arms. She felt good in his arms. He hugged her and pulled her close. She had outdone herself.

When he released her, she made her way to the bathroom. After she came out, he walked in and grabbed the cloth she'd left on the sink for him. He cleaned up and made his exit. He had every intention of coming back any chance he got.

CHAPTER 19

"You gonna be all right?" Malaina asked Joy as they approached the hotel room.

"I'm gonna be. You have no idea what the hell I feel inside," Joy said calmly. "I can deal with a lot of shit, but don't play me like that."

"I know—smile in your face while stabbing you in your back. Yeah, that's a real fucked-up move. I been there, Joy, you know it. But you can't let these fake-ass bitches break you." Malaina knocked at the door.

Joy didn't say anything. She just had a crazy look in her eyes, as if she was there in body only.

The door opened, and they walked inside to find the party jumping, a room full of women being loud, drinking, and having a good time.

Kim came out of the room where the dancers were changing. When she saw Joy, she ran up and gave her a big hug. "Where you been, girl? Why the hell you ain't been answering your phone?" she asked all giddy, feeling nice from the shooters they'd been taking. She could see something wasn't right.

Kim hugged Malaina and asked her what was wrong.

"Nothing, girl," Malaina said, shaking her head. "I'll holla at you later. Handle your business. Keep the party popping. Where the liquor? And where the entertainment?"

"They about to come out. That's what I was doing in the back," she said, walking over and dimming the lights.

When the lights went low, two dancers came out the back to the Rick Ross blasting through the box of the CD player. They began dancing for the ladies as they gathered around. All you heard was the ladies' screams as the dancers removed all their clothing, exposing themselves, allowing their long, huge dicks to swing to their every movement.

One came up on Kim and began grinding, until she fell to the floor on her back. Then he climbed on top of her and acted as if he was fucking, making the crowd of women go crazy. His dick swung back and forth, and when he stuck his ass in the air, one lady reached in from behind and grabbed it.

The other women screamed with excitement.

The other dancer inched in front of the soon-to-be bride and began gyrating his hips. He grabbed his meat and began stroking it like he was jacking it off.

She stepped back embarrassed, and as it began to swell, her mouth fell open. She put her hand over her mouth, not knowing what to do. Then another lady came up crawling and kissed his dick, before trying to put it in her mouth. She only got his head in, when he jumped back from her, realizing she was drunk and wa'n't playing.

Some women yelled, "Ooooohhhhh!" at the sight of drunken women acting out.

Joy's mind had actually started to relax as she stood back watching the nude dancers work the room. This was some new shit she'd never seen. *Leave it to Kim,* she thought.

Joy and Malaina were downing two shooters when they saw Lady and two friends walk in the party. Joy's entire demeanor changed. Her eyes tightened, and her lips poked out, showing real attitude, as the women approached with smiles and hugs.

As Lady introduced her friends, Joy walked off to the other room she'd seen Kim go into. Lady could see something was wrong with her so-called friend but never thought it could be her. Lady and her girls got drinks and returned to the floor where the dancing was going on.

Joy was gone ten minutes when Malaina saw her and Kim come out the other room to the suite.

Joy's walk was different, her facial expression was different, and she'd removed the dangling earrings she was wearing earlier. She came and stood beside them.

"So what's wrong with you, Joy? Still got man problems? You need to let that shit go tonight and have a good time." Lady couldn't understand Joy's distant attitude.

Malaina, tired of the fakery, felt she had to speak up. "You know what it is. She heard some more shit about Minke."

"Let it go. You can't keep letting that nigga mess with your head. I told you, sometimes it's best that you just leave a no-good-ass man. Let his ass be gone," Lady said like she was aggravated. "What the hell he do this time to disappoint my girl?"

Joy stared at Lady, gritting and shaking her head, her mouth twisted, becoming more enraged, not believing how sneaky she was coming off.

Malaina told her, "Girl, she found out who Minke was fuckin' around with behind her back."

"Who?" Lady asked, surprised, trying to play it off

"You, Lady. Why would you do that shit to me?" Joy asked.

Lady's eyes got wide, and her heart started pounding. "What?" was all she got out her mouth.

Joy came across her face with the box cutter Kim had given her in the room, then a right cross to her jaw that dazed Lady and shocked her friends.

Lady began swinging, and so did Joy, but with every blow Lady threw, Joy came back slicing her face until Malaina got a head full of weave and slammed her backwards to the ground and began stomping her.

The two girls with Lady grabbed Joy but quickly stopped dead in their tracks when the .380 was placed to the head of the bigger one.

The commotion stopped, and they all stared at the little, short, fat girl with chrome burner in her hand.

"Get that bitch and get the fuck out my party! Can't stand a dirty bitch! Don't make me start laying hoes down!" Kim had a stern look, heart pounding. Her finger on the trigger, she was anxious to shoot.

Lady was holding her face, her hands full of blood, as her friends eased her out the door. And the guests, the bridal party, friends, and the dancers all made their exit.

Joy and Malaina rode in silence until they reached her house.

"You gonna be all right, Joy?" Malaina asked as they sat in the car smoking, trying to calm their bodies down.

"Believe me when I tell ya. I am straight. I don't know what happen."

"Shit! I do. I knew where it was going. I couldn't look at the bitch another second and fake it. I was over it."

"I know. I saw that shit. I had just told Kim when I went to the bathroom. She came in there and cornered me, asking me what was up. I told her what was up, and she was hot. She was like, 'Confront that bitch, and let it pop.' She said she ain't really like her trifling ass no way." Joy smirked.

"I like Kim. I ain't know she get down like that. That bitch wa'n't playing. Glad she wit' us." Malaina smiled.

"Yeah, she real," Joy said, thinking about how her girl got down. "You were there as always. I know you, though. I thought you were gonna set that shit off." Joy gave Malaina a pound.

"I was going to. Then I said, 'Naw, I'm gonna give her the honors. This her shit.' Better believe she gonna remember that shit, or should I say, she gonna wear that buck fifty and recognize every day that she fucked with the wrong Brooklyn bitch. Just be careful, because you know she called Minke by now."

"I got something for his ass too."

Joy picked up her phone and called Omari. Soon as he answered, she began fake-crying. "I told him, I told him I was done," she cried.

"Told him what?" Omari asked. "Stop crying."

"I told him I was fucking with you and I didn't want him coming around. He went off. Now I don't know what to do if he come around." She continued to cry.

"I'll see you, baby. Stop crying." He hung up.

Joy then looked at Malaina and smiled. "He on his way. I'll let him deal with Minke. He said he owed him something anyway. Let them battle that shit out, and maybe afterwards, both of them simple-ass niggas will disappear out my life."

"You a trip, Joy. I guess they deserve what the hell they get, playing the games niggas play. Fuck 'em!" Malaina said, getting out the car. "Love you, Joy. Call me later. And please be careful."

"I got this. Don't nobody give a fuck about Joy. Now I'm rolling the same way. Call me when you get home," she said, making her way in the house.

***

Twenty minutes later Omari arrived at the house.

Joy answered the door in a light purple robe with nothing beneath it. He could see the print of her breasts, which was an automatic turn-on, and when he hugged her and they pressed against him, he was ready.

Omari knew the game Joy was playing but didn't care. All he wanted to do these days was to have fun. He realized she had Minke paying her bills, and was fucking the dude with the Magnum because he'd seen him bring her home several times. If Omari called, she wouldn't answer. So he knew she was full of game. So he'd got it in his mind that as long as she fucked and came off some dough, he was gonna use her as long as he could, which he knew wouldn't be long. So he came in the door ready for his pay.

Omari opened her robe and began fondling her breasts. Then he threw his fingers inside of her. She wasn't real wet, and she wasn't getting wet. That's how he knew she wasn't in the mood, for real, but he didn't care. She'd showed him how conniving she was, and he knew she was going to play it out.

They spent some time on the couch fondling each other. Then he stood up in front of her and unzipped his pants, his dick semi-hard.

"Get me hard, baby. I want you so bad," he lied.

When Joy had called, Omari had just finished fucking the girl he was living with, but she was fast asleep. She'd leaned over and took him in her mouth, leaving him speechless, only a smile on his face to show his gratitude.

Omari held Joy's head with both his hands as he stared down at her bobbing head and his meat easing in and out her mouth. *This is one thing that I would love to stick around for,* he thought. *And if fuckin' a nigga up*

*shows her I care, that's nothing, if this kind of treat-
ment continues.*

Joy's phone rang just as the head was getting good,
so he held her head snug and concentrated on cumming. It wasn't the easiest, because he had just came
where he'd just left. He held her head snugly and began fucking her face, making her gag a couple of times,
which was a humiliating move that turned him on and
sent him over the edge. Then, as he released himself,
his body jerked, and he watched cum run out the cor-
ners of her mouth.

Omari fell back on the couch, breathing hard. "Damn,
baby! You are wonderful. Don't you ever try and leave
me. I'll kill ya," he said with a smirk.

*You ain't gonna do shit but carry your punk ass,
nigga. You getting this strictly because it's part of the
plan, and I need you to carry this shit out.* Joy headed
to the bathroom.

Then she made her way back to the couch and in
Omari's arm, where they lay in deep thought, until they
dozed off.

Her phone began to ring. She ignored the first two
calls, but when it continued, she answered.

When Minke started asking her what the fuck happen, she put on a show for Omari, yelling and crying for
him to please leave her alone and hung up, knowing he
would keep calling.

It was dark when Minke came rushing through the
door with a hostile attitude. He was surprised at the
sight of Omari.

When he reached for his waist, Omari sprung on him
like a cat, rushing him before he could get his gun, scoop-
ing him up, and slamming his body to the floor in the
foyer, taking all the air out of him.

Omari pulled his burner out and started hitting Minke with the butt of the gun.

Minke was stunned but not hurt. He grabbed Omari's hand and twisted it. If Omari didn't roll with it, Minke would have broken his arm. Minke jumped to his feet, and so did Omari.

Still dazed, Minke pulled his burner and just started busting in the dark, but the shots from Omari's gun made him hit the ground and start scrambling for cover, then out the door on his knees, until he hit concrete. And he broke into a sprint, headed for his car.

The blood running down his face as he jumped in his whip told him he'd made a mistake going around there tonight. He took off after seeing the figure come out the door and the gun pointed in his direction. His life flashed before his eyes, coming to the conclusion that he'd put himself in a fucked-up situation over some pussy he wasn't even pressed for anymore.

Minke knew he wasn't in control no more, that Alecia had become one of those ignorant, wild bitches that wasn't taking his shit anymore. He wasn't about to fuck up his life because of her.

He took a deep breath thanking God he'd made it up out that house in one piece. And whatever nigga she had over there that was ready to kill him over her, he could have her. That shit wasn't worth it to him no more.

It had become all about the sex and the control he had, to be able to just fuck her any time and shit on her any time, because she had changed, lost her morals, and had no respect for herself. Minke loved her, but hated her for who she'd become, and it was not changing.

That night he came to the realization that he had to have a relationship with his kids and take of them, but he had to take a giant step back from her.

***

Two weeks had passed, and Omari had been there every day, fucking and using her every way possible.

Joy told him she needed a grand to help pay the rent, or she was gonna be ass out. Since Minke was paying it, and Omari was the cause of him not coming around, he had to come up with it, or understand that she had to work things out with Minke.

Omari ignored her, but it soon became an everyday conversation, and she stopped fucking him, just like last time, coming up with every excuse she could, the main one being, she was so worried about how she was going to come up with money, sex was the farthest thing from her mind.

Omari saw all the shit that came with Joy, and began easing his way back out the door. She was the cutest, cuddliest, and most loveable woman he'd been with, but the shit that came with her made it easy for him to step away. She was over the edge. And he made his move. Keeping his distance was the best thing for him and her.

CHAPTER 20

The day came for Joy to close on her house, and Andre sat beside her in the lawyer's office. He had it set up so that his residence was rented before hers closed, and for the last two weeks he'd been living with her. Now they were making this move into her new home, along with her kids.

Joy was so happy. For a long time, this was what she'd dreamed of. A man she could call her own, and a family she could work hard for and make prosper.

She walked out of the lawyer's office with her keys, and a feeling of self-worth and accomplishment, a feeling of not only looking complete, but being complete.

They traveled to the town house excited and in the greatest of spirits. She had purchased a home, she had reached the American dream, and nobody could tell her shit. They walked up to the door, and as she slid her key into the lock, tears formed in her eyes.

Andre knew what she was feeling. He hugged her, letting her know she'd done good.

They strolled around looking at every aspect of her new home, imagining where everything would be placed.

"You know we have to christen each and every room," he said, coming up behind her and putting his arms around her waist and kissing her neck.

Joy rested her hands on top of his and leaned her head back on his shoulder, pushing her hip on his dick and grinding. She could feel him swelling as he guided her to the edge of the loft, and braced herself.

Andre raised her skirt and pulled her panties to the side. Then he removed his meat from his jeans and slid up inside her.

Joy pushed back, spread her legs, and stuck her ass up, and he came before he could really get started.

Joy had told him that she never gave head, that she wasn't sucking no nigga dick unless he was her husband. But she felt good, and she felt close to him.

She turned around to him, dropped down, and took his nasty dick that was dripping with his cum and hers into her mouth. She sucked, gulped, and inhaled his dick like it was the last one on earth. Then she stood up and guided him to the next room by his manhood, and he followed without hesitation.

She lay back on the floor and guided him into her again. Andre was so excited, he was thrusting like a wild horse, until he burst again prematurely. She was frustrated. She wanted to cum.

She jumped up and pushed him into the master bedroom onto the floor. She pulled his pants down and jumped on his ass, so that his butt bone was in her pelvic region and pressing against her clit. And she began to grind and pump like she was fucking him, until she came, and her juices ran down his butt and in the crack of his ass.

Joy reached down between his legs and latched onto his thang then buried her face in the crack of his ass and cleaned him of all her cum, down to his balls, until his manhood was down her throat again, rising for the third time.

She then flipped him over, pulled him up, and went to the next room, where she jumped on top of him and rode him like no tomorrow. She pulled her breasts from her bra, placed a hand on both and pushed them together, and told him, "Suck 'em."

Most of the time, sucking did nothing for Joy, but the heat of the moment changed that, and she came again, collapsing on top of him.

Andre put his arms around her and embraced her every roll with passion. "I love you, girl," he said, falling back.

"I know." Joy smiled and stood up, almost stumbling from her weakness.

Andre got himself together. It was the middle of the day. Joy had taken off, and he had business. He said his good-byes, got his key, and was out.

Just as Joy was about to go out the door, her phone rang. "Hello," she answered, wondering who was calling from the unfamiliar number.

"What up?" the voice said. "Where you at?" he asked.

"My new house."

"Where?" the voice asked.

She told him, hesitant.

"I'm not far. See you in a sec."

Moments later the silver Honda Accord pulled up.

When the doorbell rang, Joy opened the door, and a smile shot across her face. As she jumped into his arms, he reached down and scooped her ass up in the air, and they embraced for what felt like forever.

"You christened this living room yet?" he asked.

"No," she answered, technically not lying, as he laid her back. "God, I missed you, Booby."

"Well, I'm home now, baby. I'm home."

Notes

Notes

Notes

HACKNEY LIBRARY SERVICES

Please return this book to any library in Hackney, on or
before the last date stamped. Fines may be charged if it is late.
Avoid fines by renewing the book (subject to it NOT being reserved).

Call the renewals line on 020 8356 2539

People who are over 60, under 18 or registered disabled
are not charged fines.

09/12

25 OCT 2012		
1 7 MAY 2013		

⊕ Hackney

PJ42014